Welcome to Big Sky Country! Where spirited men and women discover love on the range.

BEHIND CLOSED DOORS

Shhh! Can you keep a secret? The mayor has resigned and the town is in a tizzy. From fake romances to clandestine crushes, nothing in Tenacity is as it seems. The only thing these cowboys know for sure is this: they need the love of a good woman to make things right!

Cassie Trent's sister is getting married, and everyone is pressuring Cassie to bring a date. Rancher/heartthrob Graham Callahan fills the bill and then some. Cassie knows that putting her faith in a known rascal is a sure route to happily-never-after. Graham is quickly smitten, however, and is determined to prove he's worthy of Cassie's affections.

Dear Reader,

Ever sworn off love? Just think about it. Put yourself in the shoes of someone with a good reason to say no to romance and the possibility of forever with just the right person...

Both Graham Callahan and Cassie Trent are in the *never again* category when it comes to true love. Unfortunately, they each could use a little romance in their lives. Not so much for themselves, but for the sake of...appearances, I guess you could say.

In Tenacity, Montana, Cassie's got a rep as a heartbreaker. And Graham does, too. They've both grown up in this struggling community, though they've never connected until now.

Right away, they hit it off—and no, not romantically. No way. Or so they keep reminding each other.

And within days of their first real conversation, Graham has a brilliant idea that could get them both what they want. Cassie isn't sure about Graham's plan, but she is definitely tempted. And Graham's a lot of fun. It would be a deception, true, but an innocent one.

What could possibly go wrong?

I hope Graham and Cassie's story makes you laugh and root for this couple and the tough, determined people of their small, dusty hometown. And most of all, I hope it reminds you that no one is immune to love.

Happy reading, everyone,

Christine

THE MAVERICK'S DATING DEAL

CHRISTINE RIMMER

MONTANA MAVERICKS

Special thanks and acknowledgment are given to
Christine Rimmer for her contribution to
the Montana Mavericks: Behind Closed Doors miniseries.

MONTANA MAVERICKS

Recycling programs
for this product may
not exist in your area.

ISBN-13: 978-1-335-54081-2

The Maverick's Dating Deal

Copyright © 2025 by Harlequin Enterprises ULC

For questions and comments about the quality of this book, please contact us at CustomerService@Harlequin.com.

TM and ® are trademarks of Harlequin Enterprises ULC.

Harlequin Enterprises ULC
22 Adelaide St. West, 41st Floor
Toronto, Ontario M5H 4E3, Canada
www.Harlequin.com

Printed in Lithuania

MIX
Paper | Supporting
responsible forestry
FSC® C021394

Christine Rimmer came to her profession the long way around. She tried everything from acting to teaching to telephone sales. Now she's finally found work that suits her perfectly. She insists she never had a problem keeping a job—she was merely gaining "life experience" for her future as a novelist. Christine lives with her family in Oregon. Visit her at christinerimmer.com.

Books by Christine Rimmer

Harlequin Special Edition

Bravo Family Ties

Hometown Reunion
Her Best Friend's Wedding
Taking the Long Way Home
When Christmas Comes
His Best Friend's Girl

Montana Mavericks: Behind Closed Doors

The Maverick's Dating Arrangement

The Bravos of Valentine Bay

Almost a Bravo
Same Time, Next Christmas
Switched at Birth
A Husband She Couldn't Forget
The Right Reason to Marry
Their Secret Summer Family
Home for the Baby's Sake
A Temporary Christmas Arrangement
The Last One Home

Montana Mavericks: Lassoing Love

The Maverick's Surprise Son

Visit the Author Profile page at Harlequin.com for more titles.

A lifelong friend is truly one of the greatest gifts.

So this one's for my high school pal, Jackie Campbell,
who makes me laugh—and reminds me often
of the things that matter most.

Chapter One

It was a little past noon on the first day of August in the small, dusty town of Tenacity, Montana. Cassie Trent and her lifelong best friend, Victoria Woodson, were having lunch at the Silver Spur Café.

"What is it?" Vicky asked—softly, so no one at the nearby tables would hear. "Talk to me. Tell me what's going on."

Cassie didn't answer immediately. She was still trying to decide how much whining to inflict on her friend.

As Cassie thought over what to say, she gazed out the big plate glass window beside their small café table. A lone tumbleweed, blown by the summer wind, rolled down the middle of Central Avenue.

"Come on," said Vicky. "You know you want to talk about it."

Cassie ate a bite of her pulled pork sandwich and chased it down with a sip of iced tea. "Honestly, it's nothing new."

Vicky wasn't buying. "It's your mom, right?" Vicky whispered. "Just admit it, Cass. I know your mom. You're bummed because she's not going to leave you alone until you agree to bring a date to the wedding."

The wedding, Cassie thought glumly. Her older sister,

Renee, would be marrying Army veteran Miles Parker in three weeks—which was great. Cassie loved her sister dearly, and Renee couldn't wait to say *I do* to Miles. But not every woman on Earth dreamed of a ring and love everlasting. "Really, Vick. It is what it is and you don't need to hear it."

Vicky sighed, glanced at her phone and put it back, face down, on the edge of their table. "I just thought you might want to vent." She eased a bit of bacon from her BLT and munched it without enthusiasm. When she glanced up and saw Cassie watching her, she made an effort to smile, but it didn't quite happen. Because Vicky seemed every bit as miserable and preoccupied as Cassie was.

The two of them usually enjoyed their occasional lunches at the Silver Spur Café. Cassie looked forward to catching up with Vicky, laughing over this or that, sometimes reminiscing the way longtime friends will do.

But today Cassie just wasn't into it. She *was* feeling grim about the wedding. Her mom's constant nagging was getting her down. Vicky looked equally gloomy—and how many times had she glanced at her phone?

Several. Vicky had major family problems and was probably anticipating an urgent call from her mom or her brother, Brent.

Clifford Woodson, Vicky's dad, had recently stepped down as Tenacity's mayor—a position he'd held for more than two decades, and also one he hadn't given up willingly. The painful truth was that Mayor Woodson's unscrupulous behavior had finally caught up with him.

Not only was the mayor in disgrace, but Vicky's mom was now believed to have stolen a huge sum of money from the town coffers fifteen years before. June Woodson, it turned out, had been in love with another man at the time. She'd stolen the money as part of her plan to run away with her lover.

When the money vanished, municipal projects were tabled, and one small business after another folded. Many townspeople attributed Tenacity's financial downturn to the loss of the money June Woodson had taken.

Vicky, still waiting for Cassie to talk about *her* problems, whispered sternly, "Come on. Spill."

"You sure?"

"Talk to me. Now. Tell me all about it."

Cassie gave it up. "You're right. *Everybody's* after me. You know how they are. They all think I need a man to put a ring on it. It doesn't matter how many times I remind them that I've been in love more than once—and when the moment of truth was upon me, I choked." So far in her twenty-seven years of life, Cassie had turned down three sincere marriage proposals. "I said no to three fine men—and you know why I did it, too."

Vicky did know. "Because the single life is the life for you."

"Exactly. Why can't my mother see that?"

Vicky reached across the table and patted the back of her hand. "I'm with you. I do understand…"

"Thanks. It helps to hear you say it. Because, believe me, you are the *only* one who gets it. It doesn't matter how many times I explain that I have given up men, no one takes me seriously. Especially not my mom. She acts like I'm just being stubborn, you know? Like if she keeps after me long enough, I'm going snap out of it, grab the nearest single man and drag him to the altar."

Vicky shifted in her chair. It was a definite tell. She was about to say something she knew Cassie wouldn't like. "Listen, I get your frustration…"

Cassie let out a big sigh. "But…?"

"Well, Cass, it's just a date." She leaned in close again and lowered her voice another notch. "You don't have to marry the guy."

Cassie tried really hard not to roll her eyes. "That's what *you* think. My mom wants me married, and she's not going to stop until I've got a ring on my finger. A date for Renee's wedding is just the first step down a slippery slope."

"Honestly, I think you're making a big deal out of—"

"Uh-uh. No, I'm not. I don't want a date for the wedding. I don't want a date under any circumstances. I'm done dating. Over. Finished. Through. Have I made myself clear?"

"Okay, okay." Her BFF put up both hands in surrender.

"Good, then."

Vicky took a bite of her sandwich. As she chewed, she seemed thoughtful. And then she asked, "Do you believe that Miles and your sister have what it takes to make it for the long haul?"

Thinking about Renee and Miles actually lightened Cassie's mood. She smiled. "You know what? I do. They're good together and they really love each other."

"I hope you're right." Shaking her head, Vicky added mournfully, "Because forever is a long, long time…"

"Hey…" Cassie held her friend's gaze.

"Hmm?"

"Your turn." Cassie pressed, "Tell me what's on *your* mind. Whatever it is, I'm here and I'm listening." When Vicky looked away with a sad little shrug, Cassie caught her hand and whispered insistently, "Just talk to me. Come on…"

Vicky met her gaze again. "You asked for it." She made

a mournful little sound and whispered, "The inevitable is finally upon us. After more than thirty miserable years together, my mom has pulled the plug. She filed for divorce from my dad."

They'd both known it was coming. Still, the reality hit hard. "Oh, honey…"

"My dad's on the rampage, blaming everybody but himself. As usual. And Brent and me? We're the town pariahs."

"No. Vicky, that's not true."

"Yes, it is." Vicky's voice was flat. "You know it is."

"Uh-uh. No one can blame you or your brother for what your parents did."

"Sure they can," she muttered.

"*Who* blames you or Brent? Tell me. I'll have a long talk with them."

"I'm just saying, people look at me funny now…"

Cassie gave her friend's hand another squeeze. "You are not to blame. And, Vick, there really is something going on with you, isn't there?"

"What? No…"

"Yeah, there is—something beyond the old scandal and the revelation that your mom stole the money. Something beyond your mom finally filing for divorce."

Vicky looked away with a shrug.

Cassie kept after her. "Just tell me. Whatever it is, we can work it out together."

For a long count of ten, Vicky said nothing. Then she shook her head. "It's just… I'm sad, Cass. Very, very sad. I mean, it seems like everyone in this town is at least partly complicit in what happened back then."

"Everyone? That's not so. You're upset and you're exaggerating."

"Think about it. Why is it that no one ever questioned the ridiculous story my dad made up?" Fifteen years ago, after Vicky's mom stole thousands of dollars from the town accounts, Vicky's dad had wrongly accused straight-A student Barrett Deroy, Jr. of the theft. At the time, the people of Tenacity had believed that lie.

"Hmm." Cassie nodded. "You know, you do kind of have a point about that. It never made any real sense that a high school student could get access to the town's money."

"No kidding." Vicky's whisper was weighted with scorn. "It makes no sense today and it made no sense fifteen years ago, yet somehow, back then, everyone believed my dad's lie."

When the scandal broke, the Deroys were so worried that their son would go to prison, they took Barrett, Jr. and skipped town.

But the real story, which had only come out recently, was that Vicky's dad had accused Barrett, Jr. to punish his wife for her affair—with Barrett, Sr. Now, with everyone in town knowing that Mayor Clifford Woodson had wrongly implicated an innocent young man, Vicky's dad had been forced to step down from office.

Across their small table, Vicky's cheeks were flushed and her eyes wet with barely controlled tears. "I just… Oh, Cass. I don't know what to do…"

"What to do? What *can* you do? Nothing that's happened is in any way your fault…"

Vicky looked stricken. She hung her head. "Really, Cass. There's more to this than you…" Right then, her phone rang. Vicky turned it over again to look at the screen. "Oh, no. It's my mom. I'm sorry, I have to go."

"But Vick…"

"Really, I do have go. I hate to run out on you, but it's a hard time for her and she needs me right now."

Cassie nodded reluctantly. "Okay, then. Do what you have to do."

Vicky whipped out her wallet, dropped some bills on the table, scooped up her phone and pushed back her chair. "Talk soon, I promise." She turned for the door.

Wondering what her best friend was keeping from her, Cassie watched her go. She wanted to help, but how could she do that until Vicky came clean?

Resigned, Cassie picked up her sandwich for another bite—just as two friends from high school appeared at her side.

Larinda Peach and Roslyn Ainsly were both married, with small children. They wanted to know how the wedding preparations were going—and to quiz Cassie on which "lucky" guy would be her date for the big event.

Cassie chewed and swallowed, smiled and nodded. She said that the wedding was going to be beautiful and she couldn't wait to watch her big sister walk down the aisle. As for who her date would be, she nibbled more barbecue and said, "It's a secret."

"Why?" Roslyn demanded.

"Well…" By then, Cassie was feeling a bit contrary and more than a little frustrated. Because so what if she had a date for her sister's wedding or not?

Roslyn and Larinda were as bad as her mom, prying into her nonexistent love life like they had a right to know her private business.

"Tell us!" Larinda begged.

"We'll keep your secret," whispered Roslyn.

"Yes!" insisted Larinda. "Tell us who he is and we won't say a word to anyone."

"Honestly, you guys. There's no one."

Roslyn frowned in puzzlement. "You just said it was a secret."

"Yeah, well. It *is* a secret. And the secret is, there's no one."

Larinda chuckled. "Oh, now. You know we don't believe that."

Cassie cast a glance around the busy café. People *were* watching—and then looking quickly away when she caught them at it. If she came up with a name, it would be all over town by dinnertime. But she wouldn't do that—because there *was* no mystery man.

She might, however, be getting annoyed enough with the situation to start saying things that weren't true. No, she shouldn't tell a lie and she knew it. But if people just had to be all up in her business, she would definitely find a way to get them off her back.

"The thing is…" She nibbled a French fry—and crossed the line between truth and fiction. "I'm kind of seeing someone."

"Who?" asked Roslyn breathlessly.

Cassie tried her best to look regretful. "Can't say."

"But why not?" inquired Larina.

"Because as of right now, we're keeping it low-key."

"Why?" Roslyn frowned down at her.

"Well, it's new, this thing between us." And it was. So new it hadn't even happened. "We're taking it slow—and besides, my…friend isn't sure he can make it to the wedding."

"Oh, no," mourned Larinda. "He *has* to come to the wedding."

Cassie put on a glum look. "You know how it is, Larinda. Sadly, sometimes things just don't work out the way we want them to."

Roslyn patted Cassie's shoulder. "It *will* work out. You'll see. He'll be there."

Cassie nodded solemnly. "Oh, I do hope so…" No doubt about it. She was going to hell for being a shameless liar.

Larinda and Roslyn made more sympathetic noises and asked her to please reach out if she needed someone to talk to. Cassie lied some more and promised she would absolutely turn to them when the longing to confide became too strong to bear.

They'd just left her in peace when one of her mother's friends, Myrna Ripley, came by. "Cassie, honey. It's so good to see you…"

"Myrna, hi…" Cassie got up and hugged the older woman. Like Cassie's high school friends, Myrna asked about Renee's wedding. Cassie brought her up to speed.

And then Myrna said, "I know you're…on your own lately. But of course the maid of honor needs a date."

"Yes, Myrna," Cassie replied with a stiff little smile. "But don't worry. I have the date situation handled." *Because I'm not going to bring a date.* "And I want you to confess…"

"Confess what?" Myrna tried to look innocent.

"Myrna, I know my mom put you up to this."

Myrna widened her eyes. "Honey, honestly. Your mother did no such thing."

"You're sure?"

"Of course, I'm sure!"

Cassie stifled a sigh. "Okay, Myrna. Whatever you say—and as for needing a date, I don't. I really don't."

Just like Larinda and Roslyn, Myrna patted Cassie's

shoulder. "Yes, you do, sweetie. And you need to get on it. The wedding is coming up fast."

"Yes. I know. But, um, you see, it all depends…"

Myrna leaned closer. "On what?"

Cassie pretended to be deep in thought. In reality, she was actually wondering if she ought to fall back on the imaginary boyfriend story. Could it get her through the wedding? Maybe. When the boyfriend never showed, she could tell her mother that it simply hadn't worked out with the guy…

Right now, with Myrna looming over her, an imaginary boyfriend seemed more and more like a viable plan. Every time her mom got on her about a date for the wedding, she could claim that the guy was trying to juggle his schedule, that he was doing everything he could to make it work…

"Cassie, honey…?"

Blinking, Cassie refocused on Myrna. "Sorry. You were saying?"

"Well, sweetie, it all depends on what?"

Cassie had no idea. "So many things, Myrna. It all depends on so many things. Life's a mystery, no doubt about it."

Myrna peered at her more closely. "Are you all right, dear?"

"I'm just great, never better."

A moment later, Myrna finally gave up quizzing Cassie and moved on.

And a good thing, too. By then, all she wanted was out of the Silver Spur as quickly as possible. She signaled Eileen, the server, for the check.

And right then, Graham Callahan sauntered in.

Tall, lean, hot and handsome with a devilish gleam in

his dark eyes, Graham was the kind of guy who made an immediate impression on everyone he met. Everybody loved him, even though he had a well-deserved reputation for breaking a long chain of feminine hearts.

He owned a ranch in partnership with his three equally tall, handsome brothers. Today, he carried what looked like a pile of flyers, and he was wearing his best killer grin.

"Here you go." Eileen set down Cassie's check and cleared off the remains of her lunch as Graham started making the rounds of the restaurant.

He shook hands and passed out the flyers as he moved from table to table. "I've got big news," he announced loud enough for everyone in the place to hear. "Now that Mayor Woodson has stepped down, I'm putting my hat in the ring to take his place!" And with that, he whipped the hat off his head and waved it around before pressing it to his heart.

By then, he stood in the center of the restaurant. "And I hope you will all put your trust in me!"

The little speech was met with cheers and applause. Privately, Cassie wondered why everyone seemed to think that Graham Callahan was mayoral material. The guy might be a total smoke show. But good looks and way too much charm hardly qualified him to run their troubled township.

Then again, she thought, *why not*? Graham was enthusiastic and upbeat. After the backbiting and dirty tricks Clifford Woodson had put their town through, the citizens of Tenacity could use a change of pace.

As that thought popped into her head, Graham spotted her watching him. That sexy grin widened. He was coming her way.

Graham had to be—what? In his early thirties by now the way she figured it. He'd been four or five years ahead of Cassie in school. She watched him weave his way through the tables toward her and thought how, until this moment, the two of them had never shared more than a nod and a smile in passing.

But this was Tenacity. Everybody knew far too much about everybody else—even the people they'd never exchanged more than a few words with.

He stood across the small table from her. "Cassie Trent. How are you?"

"Just fine, Graham. You?"

He had a dangerous gleam in those gorgeous dark eyes. "From where I'm standing, the view is downright beautiful."

She gave him a cool smile. "So nice of you to say so."

He tapped the back of the empty chair across from her. "Mind if I join you?"

She started to say that she was just leaving. But then again...

Okay, Graham was brash. And a little bit over-the-top. But his smile was real and his outlook so positive.

Maybe a little of that optimism would rub off on her. Because seriously, her friend Vicky was downright miserable and completely unwilling to talk about it. And then there was Cassie's own frustration with the constant pressure from all sides to get herself a man and settle down.

Right now, the idea of hanging out for a while with the hunky, cheerful mayoral candidate felt like just what the doctor ordered.

"Have a seat, Graham."

He pulled out the chair and dropped into it. "You know, Cassie. I really like your attitude."

She almost laughed. "Which attitude is that?"

"I like that you're doubtful."

"About…?"

"Me."

She wasn't sure she understood. "Okay, so… I have a doubtful attitude about you and you *like* it?"

"Exactly." He put the stack of flyers on the table and set his hat on top of them.

Right then, Eileen reappeared. "What'll you have, Graham?"

"Steak sandwich and whatever's on tap."

"You got it." Eileen turned to Cassie. "How about you, Cassie? Chocolate Lava Cake?" Eileen grinned. "You know you need it."

"I'm good, thanks. Maybe next time…"

As Eileen trotted off, Graham pulled a flyer out from under his hat, set it on the table—and spun it around so it was facing her. "So I get it," he said. "You're just not sure I'm mayoral material."

She glanced down at the flyer. It was a headshot of Graham framed in a red, white and blue graphic. "Graham Callahan for Mayor!" the flyer proclaimed. "Your Vote, Your Voice!"

"Okay, I'll bite," she said. "The truth is, we need someone not only trustworthy but steady and serious to run this town. The way I see it, you're not exactly…" She got stuck there because he was a good guy, really, and she hesitated to call him a lightweight.

"*That*," he said, pointing his finger at her.

"Er, what?"

"Whatever you're not saying. It's why you and I have to talk. Because you're just the kind of voter I need to convince. It's clear that you're skeptical of my readiness for the job, and that's why I want you to lay it on me, Cassie. I want you to tell me what you think I need to do to show this town I'm the man to be their mayor."

She met his eyes and didn't blink. "Be careful what you ask for, Graham Callahan…"

He smirked. "Bring it on."

"Alrighty then. For starters, I'm guessing you're used to people saying yes to you. But, Graham, good looks can only take a person so far in this world."

"Hmm. So you think I'm good-looking?"

She almost laughed. He was so relentlessly upbeat, not to mention egotistical in the most attractive way. "Yes, I do think you're good-looking. And your looks and charm might win you the election, but that doesn't mean you're qualified to do the job."

He seemed to take zero offense at her assessment. Instead, he laughed, a carefree sort of laugh, the laugh of a confident man. "Cassie. I wish that everyone was as direct as you are—and you're right. I have no experience in government. But I do know economics and I have solid ideas as to how to put this town back in the black."

She vaguely remembered he'd gone to college in Seattle. "Economics, huh?"

He nodded. "I got my MBA at UW."

"Wow. Fancy."

He looked at her sideways. "Are you mocking me?"

"No, Graham, of course not."

"I'm not sure I believe you." At least he was smiling when he said that.

"It's just, you come across as fun and easygoing. I never realized you were an economist."

"Yeah, well. Economists can be fun, too. And I'm one of the fun ones." He winked at her. "In fact, I worked as a financial analyst at a major construction firm for three years before I moved back home."

"Why?"

"Pardon me?"

"Why did you move back home?"

"I realized I didn't want to live anywhere else," he replied. She believed him, as far as it went. But something in those dark eyes told her there was more to the story. Before she could ask him for the real reason he'd come home to stay, he went on. "I know my way around a budget—and a financial statement. I'm running on fiscal transparency and responsibility. I think this town deserves a fresh start, and we won't get that if we just elect another guy who says *trust me* and then blames an innocent kid when the town accounts come up empty." Eileen set a mug of beer in front of him.

"Thank you," he said as he pushed the flyers to the side. Eileen bustled away and those dark eyes settled on Cassie again. "So here's a question. Would you consider stepping up as my deputy mayor?"

"Whoa!" Cassie laughed. "Graham, I'm a rancher, not a politician, thank you very much." She peered at him more closely. "Wait a minute. You're serious?"

"I am." He wasn't smiling now. "And that you have to ask if I mean what I'm saying, well, that's my biggest problem." He lowered his voice for her ears alone. "Everybody's always happy to see me, but no one thinks I'm serious about this. Cassie, I do care about this town, and I think I could make a real difference if only voters would give me a chance."

"But, Graham…" She hesitated. Because just to lay it right out there, to say, *You're a hot, flirty cowboy break-*

*ing hearts right and left, and nobody's going to choose
you to run this town...*

Well, it might be true, but it was also kind of harsh.

Cassie found she didn't want to be harsh to Graham.
Now that she was having her first real conversation with
the man, she found him to be sweet, charming, sincere—
and well-meaning, too.

She made an effort to tell the truth in a gentle way. "My
point is, you don't come across as very serious. A candidate for mayor really should be thoughtful and steady."

"And I will be. You'll see." Graham glanced around
them. Right now, their neighbors at the other tables
seemed to be minding their own business. He asked,
very quietly, "This is about my reputation as a hound
dog, right?"

She leaned in and whispered back, "I never said you
were a hound dog."

"Fair enough. But let me just clarify something, would
you, please?"

"All right."

"Well, as for the women I've dated here in town, I've
always made it clear that I'm never getting serious, that
if a woman is looking for love and a wedding ring, she's
not going to get that from me."

She folded her arms and kept her voice low. "Honestly.
This conversation has gotten dangerously personal. I don't
know what to say to you."

"The truth, Cassie. Just tell me the truth."

"Okay, then, Graham. The truth is that telling women
you won't ever get serious hasn't really helped. They still
fall for you and end up with their hearts broken. I mean,
come on. You're just like my brother Ryder. I think you've
dated every unattached woman in town."

"Not true." His dark eyes gleamed. "Think about it, Cassie. I've never dated you."

Laughing, Cassie shook her head. "See what I mean? It's like a knee-jerk reaction with you. You see a woman, you put a move on her."

"But I'm not putting a move on you." Was he serious? She honestly couldn't tell.

Eileen bustled up to the table again, this time with Graham's steak sandwich. He thanked her, and she rushed off to deliver more orders. Graham shook out his napkin and glanced up at Cassie. "Mind if I…?"

She waved away his hesitation with a flick of her wrist. "Eat."

He dug in. For a minute or two, they were both silent.

When he finished chewing and swallowed, he drank from his beer and said, "Truth is, Cassie Trent, I find you a little bit intimidating. Always have."

"How could you find me intimidating? You don't know me. This is the first time we've ever actually talked."

"Cassie. It's Tenacity. Just because we've never shared a conversation before doesn't mean we don't know way too much about each other. And I know about you, Cassie Trent. You call them as you see them."

She thought how she'd considered not mentioning his reputation as a heartbreaker because she didn't want to treat him harshly—and yet, in the end, she'd called him on it, anyway. "You're right. I do say what's on my mind."

He munched a steak fry. "Thank you for your honesty. You should run for town council. I need you on my team."

"You actually have a team?"

He glissaded right by her question. "I really would like to nominate you for my deputy mayor."

"Graham. Don't get ahead of yourself. First, win the

election. Then you can decide who to put forward as your deputy mayor."

"You do seem to know a lot about how things work in town government."

"Not particularly. But I..." She thought of Vicky again—and hoped she was okay. "Well, I do have a dear friend whose dad used to be the mayor."

He set down his half-eaten sandwich. "That's right. You're close with Victoria Woodson, aren't you?"

"Yes, I am." She said it defiantly.

He picked up on her attitude and put up both hands. "Hey, now. What'd I do?"

"Nothing. So far. But some people in town judge my friend and her brother because of what their parents have done."

He looked at her steadily. "Not me."

"Good. Because Vicky is my dearest friend and she is innocent of all blame in this mess her parents created."

"Gotcha," he said with a nod. "And I meant what I said. You seem to have a good head on your shoulders and to know a lot about how this town is run. All I'm asking is that you think about my offer. If nothing else, say you'll be a sounding board for me in the race, help me to better understand what I'm up against."

"No, thanks." She grabbed her check and got up to go.

"Tip's on me!" Graham said with a wink. He fished a bill from his pocket and dropped it in the middle of the table. It was a twenty.

Cassie gave him the side-eye. "I see your plan. You're going to win the election one tip at a time."

"Hey, Eileen deserves a little extra." He grinned up at her, and she couldn't help grinning right back. It was always a good sign when a man acknowledged and appreciated the people around him who made his life easier. Graham Callahan was a sweetheart—and a real hunk to boot.

"Everything tasty?" asked Eileen at the register as Cassie paid for her meal.

"Perfect. Thank you."

As Cassie turned for the door, she spotted former deputy mayor Marty Moore sitting a few feet away. Marty had stepped up as acting mayor when Vicky's dad left office in disgrace, and now Marty was running to claim the job permanently.

"Hello, Miss Cassie Trent." Beneath his bushy walrus mustache, Marty's fleshy mouth quirked in what could have been a smile but looked more like a sneer.

"Mister Marty Moore." She refused to call him by his temporary title. He might be the mayor for now, but Cassie was certain he'd be voted out come the election in November. Maybe in favor of Graham, who had his shortcomings, but really did seem to care about Tenacity.

Marty Moore only cared about the fellow he saw when he looked in the mirror. The acting mayor was just one of those guys—the smug, borderline creepy sort. The look in his eyes alone made her uncomfortable. And had he been listening in on her conversation with Graham?

Well, so what? It was Tenacity, after all, she reminded herself. Everybody was always sticking their noses in everybody else's business. She wasn't letting Marty get to her. Not now.

And not ever.

Chapter Two

The five-month-old Angus calf weighed a good four hundred pounds and was very unhappy. It stood in the middle of Callahan Creek mooing for its mama. From the bank, Izzy, Graham's border collie, let out a whine of impatience.

Before the dog could launch herself into the stream, Graham commanded, "Stay." With a whine of disappointment, Izzy dropped to her haunches.

Graham urged his horse down the bank and into the water. The calf just stood there bawling, watching the horse come closer. "Git, now!" Graham clicked his tongue. "Go on! Git on up out of here…"

"You tell him, Graham!" shouted his brother Archer from the dry bank on the far side of the creek.

Graham ignored him and shifted his weight in the saddle so his mount moved sideways, hemming in the stubborn calf. It didn't take long before the critter surrendered and scrambled up the bank toward Archer.

Graham whistled for Izzy, who jumped in and swam across as Archer and Graham got behind the rebel calf, driving it forward. The calf took off, bellyaching all the way, to where its mama stood calmly nipping up the short grass.

Finally, with a little urging from Graham, cow and calf trotted over to join the rest of the small herd of strays the brothers had rounded up. Working them from either side, with Izzy taking up the drag, Graham and Archer drove them through the canyon after which the family ranch, Callahan Canyon, had been named.

Once they emerged onto open land again, it wasn't far to the west pasture and fresh grazing. Archer went on ahead to open the pasture gate and then circled back to help Graham and Izzy push the cattle through.

The cows and their calves were happily munching the thick grass when the brothers and Izzy left the pasture. Graham rode through the gate first, Izzy at his side. Archer followed, dismounting long enough to shut the gate behind them.

By then it was almost noon. They headed back through the canyon the way they'd come.

Earlier, they'd been talking about the race for mayor. Now, as they ambled along, Archer picked up the conversation where they'd left off. "I meant what I said, Graham. Picturing you behind that big desk in the mayor's office..." Archer let his voice trail off as he slowly shook his head.

Graham kept his mouth shut. He figured whatever his brother said next wouldn't be all that flattering, so why encourage him?

Finally, after a silence long enough to drive a wagon train through, Archer finished with a shrug. "I can't see it, you know? It's not you. It's just...out there, that's what it is."

"Okay, brother. I'll play along. Out *where*, exactly?"

For no discernable reason, Archer clicked his tongue at his horse and readjusted his hat, lifting it and then clamping it tighter onto his head. At twenty-nine, Archer was the youngest of the four Callahan brothers. He was tall and lean, same as Graham. Archer loved the ranching life. He didn't get why any man would want to work in town.

"Well, I mean, why would you even want to be mayor? You'd spend way too much time at the town hall, taking meetings and making big decisions. That's not you."

"So then, what you're saying is that you don't think I can handle the job."

Archer shrugged. "It's a desk job with a bunch of official duties thrown in. You had a desk job in Seattle, remember? And that didn't work out so great for you."

Their horses' hooves clattered along the rocky canyon floor as Graham looked over at his brother and waited until Archer met his eyes. Then he said, "I did leave Seattle, yeah. But it wasn't because I hated my desk job." He kept his tone mild, with a hint of humor.

Archer got the message anyway. "Sorry," he said sincerely. "I didn't mean to poke at a sore spot."

"It's okay. But what I'm getting at is that I was a damn fine financial analyst, just in case no one ever told you."

"I know, I know. You're good with money, and in this town and this economy, we're all grateful for that." A lot of ranches were going under these days, but with his brothers' hard work and Graham's ability to manage what they brought in, Callahan Canyon operated in the black.

And Archer wasn't finished. "But Graham, when you came home, you said you were glad to get out on the land again, that you were sick to death of spending your working life staring at a laptop screen."

"And I meant that. I do love being home. But I might have exaggerated my supposed hatred for the corporate world just a tad."

"Fair enough. I still can't picture you running town meetings and giving speeches. I mean, think about it. You'd have to kiss babies, too, you know."

"Hey." Graham shrugged. "I'll bet I can run a meeting and kiss a cute baby with the best of them. Maybe I'll surprise you. And after all those years of that crooked stuffed shirt, Woodson, followed by Marty Moore, who couldn't crack a sincere smile if you paid him to do it… Well, it wouldn't hurt for the mayor to be a good guy with an easy-going attitude for a change. I'm planning to bring a whole new, upbeat, friendly, open-minded approach to the job."

"That is, *if* you're elected," Archer said with a smart-ass grin.

"Got to think positive, brother!" Graham reminded him.

Archer shrugged. "I just don't want you to get ahead of yourself. You need to face the facts."

"Which facts are those?"

"Graham, there are going to be people who don't take your bid for office seriously. You'll have to prove to them that you're for real. You're going to need a…what do they call it? A platform. People will want to know what you're planning to do once you're in office. And most of all, you're going to need to convince them that you're not going to get tired of the job the same way you got tired of Celia and Jacqueline and Suzie and—"

"Enough." Graham tipped his head back and watched a hawk soar across the wedge of clear blue sky between the canyon walls to either side of them. He was thinking about Cassie Trent and their conversation yesterday. She'd brought up his long list of girlfriends, too. He needed to make a plan to minimize his reputation as a guy who played fast and loose with a woman's heart.

Fast and loose...

Was that really what he'd done, taken advantage of the women he'd dated after he moved back home from Seattle?

The more he thought back on it, well, he wasn't too proud of his own behavior over the past few years. Yeah, he'd always been clear with the women he dated that it was just for fun and just for now. But Cassie had it right. When a woman wanted one thing and a man wanted another, well, misunderstandings were way too likely to occur. He needed to do better, to show his hometown that he could be reliable, caring and serious.

But how?

Archer said, "You need to show that you're ready to settle down and be a grown-up, ready to put that mess with Serena behind you."

Serena. Even after five years, he still hated just hearing her name. "And how am I going to do that?"

"I don't know." But then Archer suggested, "You could maybe find a girlfriend and stick with her this time."

That is never going to happen, a bitter voice in his head grumbled. He'd had his heart ripped out and stomped flat once. That was way more than enough. "Sorry, but the plain fact is I'm never going to the settling-down place again."

"We'll see about that," said his brother. "Yeah, okay. Maybe you're not ready right now—"

"Try *never*, Archer. I will *never* be ready."

"Keep telling yourself that," said Archer knowingly, like he was suddenly the older, wiser brother. "Someday the *right* woman will lasso your heart. You'll go down smiling."

"Not going to happen."

Archer went on as though Graham hadn't spoken. "Wait and see—and as for right now, if you want to be mayor, you need to show the people of Tenacity that you're more than just a smooth talker with a handsome face."

Graham opened his mouth to argue some more. But then he shut it without a word. Because what Archer had just said was pretty much the same thing Cassie Trent had told him.

He needed to put some effort into showing folks in town that he could get serious. He had to find a way to reassure his future constituents that he could be trusted to look out for them, to clean up the fiscal mess Clifford Woodson had left behind and point the way to a new prosperity for their town.

A single guy who never went out with any woman more than twice did not come across as dependable. Graham needed to face that issue, to deal with it head-on—and come to think of it, he knew just the woman to help him do that…

"What are you grinning about all of a sudden?" Archer demanded as he guided his gelding around a rocky outcropping.

Graham glanced up at the clear blue sky. "It's a beautiful day and we're almost home," he said, smiling even wider. "What's not to grin about?"

As they emerged from the canyon, the main house appeared ahead of them. His own house was over a rise farther out. In the distance, beyond a tall stand of mature cottonwoods, the barn, corral, horse pasture and sheds baked beneath the midday sun.

"You're planning something," his brother accused.

"Nah." Graham played innocent for all he was worth.

"Yeah, you are."

"No, I'm not." By then they were grinning at each other.

Archer warned, "Whatever it is, I hope you know what you're doing."

"Trust me," said Graham.

Archer scoffed—and left it at that.

On Monday, three days after her encounter with Graham Callahan at the café, Cassie was at home on Stargazer Ranch, out in the hay meadow not far from the main ranch house.

She'd just started painting the white side of the main barn red to match the rest of the structure when she heard a vehicle approach. Turning, she spotted a dusty black crew cab. The truck came rolling down the two-track road that ran along the fence line out there on the other side of the meadow from the barn. The big truck stopped almost parallel with where she stood, roller in hand. The driver's door swung open.

When Graham Callahan stepped out, Cassie grinned— because after their conversation last Friday, she'd decided she liked him. Also, finding out what he was up to would be a welcome break from the task at hand.

He swept off his hat and waved it at her. "Hey, Cassie!"

Bending, she set her roller in the paint tray and then jogged across the meadow to meet him at the fence. "What a surprise." She offered her hand. They shook over the top rail.

Today he was dressed very much like she was, in an old shirt, faded jeans and a straw Resistol hat. He smelled fresh, like he'd just had a shower—after a long morning's work at Callahan Canyon, no doubt.

Ignoring the little flutter in her middle as her palm met

his, she assumed he must have come to drum up votes from the Trent family. "My father and brother are out in one of the far pastures," she said, "and my sister, Renee, is off in her retrofitted school bus, making the rounds."

"Good to know. How's that dog grooming business going for Renee?"

"Great—but as I said, she's not here right at the moment. However, if you want to talk politics with my mom, just follow the road to the main house. She's working in her garden, so go on through the front gate and take the garden path around to the back of the house."

He swiped off his hat again and raked his fingers through his thick, straight hair. "Truth is, Cassie, it's you I came to see."

"So you're asking for *my* vote, then?"

"Well, it's a little more complicated than that. Got a few minutes?"

She shot a thumb back over her shoulder at the barn. "Mind if I paint while we talk?"

"Not at all—and hey, if you happen to have an extra brush I'd be glad to pitch in."

She tipped her head to the side and studied the chiseled planes of his face. "I should say no way, that it's not your job to paint our barn. But I just painted that side of the barn two months ago and I'm really annoyed with myself that here I am doing it all over again."

That slow grin of his? Somebody should bottle it and sell it. "So then let me help. The job will go faster."

"You really don't have to do that."

"No, I don't. But I *want* to help."

"Okay, Graham. You asked for it."

There was that grin again. "Lead the way."

A few minutes later, she'd provided him with his own paint tray and roller. They set to work side by side.

"Let me guess," he said as he rolled on the red paint. "You were going to paint the barn white but you did this one wall and changed your mind...?"

"Nope." She dipped up more paint and went to work with a vengeance.

"Then...?"

She sighed. "I had the brilliant idea to use this wall of the barn as a movie screen. I planned to buy a projector, set up a concession stand offering popcorn and cold drinks, and sell tickets to outdoor movies on Friday nights all summer long."

He sent her an approving glance. "That's a good idea."

She sighed some more. "I thought so, too. I even bought what they call projector paint at three hundred bucks a gallon."

"So you painted this side of the barn for your movie screen..."

"Yes, I did—too bad I did that *before* doing my research. When I finally started reading up on my little summer project, I learned that you can't sell tickets to movies without paying licensing fees and those fees run several hundred bucks per showing."

"Uh-oh," he said. Beneath the short sleeve of his worn T-shirt, his hard arm flexed with each stroke of the roller.

"Exactly," she grumbled. "I was picturing folks bringing blankets, sitting on the grass—real basic, you know. And I would be showing older movies so it wouldn't cost me all that much. A side hustle, for fun and a little bit of profit. I was thinking five bucks a head—that it would be worth it if I could scare up fifty or sixty customers each movie night. But then I found out I would need more people than that just to pay the licensing fees." She rolled on more paint. "Anyway. So much for summer movies out under the wide Montana sky at Stargazer Ranch."

"Too bad. It's a cool idea."

"I thought so, too, but now I'm just bitter about it. And my mom's been after me for a month and a half now to paint this wall the same color as the rest of the barn again, given that I'm not going to use it for a movie screen. I'm telling you, Graham, it's hard when a good dream has to die."

"That it is," he agreed, still dipping up the paint and rolling it on his side of the barn wall.

From the goat pen at the far end of the meadow toward the main gate, two of her miniature Nubian milk goats bleated in unison. She glanced their way and grinned. They loved to stick their noses through the four-inch spaces in the woven-wire fence that penned them in.

"Settle down, ladies!" she called to them.

In response, they bleated some more.

When she turned back to Graham, he was watching her with a bemused sort of smile on his gorgeous face. "Goats, huh?"

"Yup. Milk goats, as a matter of fact. Now, that's a successful side hustle. Goat milk is delicious and it's healthier than cow's milk. Here on the ranch, we all drink the milk my goats produce. I sell the extra. I also sell most of the kids. I can usually get a hundred each for the doelings. For the little bucks, I try for eighty, but as a rule I end up going down to fifty. On average, each of my milk does makes me a minimum of seven hundred fifty a year—plus, as animals go, they're not all that difficult to take care of."

He was grinning. "You love them."

"Yes, I do. If they grow up around people, they're

funny and sweet, especially if you bottle-feed them. They bond with you."

"Are you saving up your side hustle money for something special?" The way he looked at her—admiring and also amused… He made her feel all bubbly inside. She probably needed to keep a lid on her reaction to him. The guy was far too charming for her peace of mind.

"No," she said softly. "Not for anything in particular. But you know how it is. It never hurts to have a little extra put away for lean times."

"I hear you." He said it quietly. Kind of seriously. In Tenacity, most everybody knew what it was like to scrape and struggle to get by.

The look they shared went on for far too long. And then, as though by silent mutual agreement, they turned back to the barn and got to work again.

A little while later, she brought out a brush and a forty-foot extension ladder. He volunteered to get up there on the ladder and cut in under the eaves—no easy task by hand. She felt more than a little bit guilty letting him do that and tried to object. He insisted. Once that was done, he took his roller and a tray of paint up there to fill what he'd cut in. The tray fit just fine on the ladder's detachable utility shelf.

He surprised her. Four hours after he drove up and stopped by the fence, he was still there, and together they'd finished the first coat.

She stood at the foot of the ladder and looked up at him. "Enough. Come on down. We're done for the day."

"Just a minute," he replied as he set the roller in the tray.

She waited at the foot of the ladder, staring up at him. He seemed to be to be studying his work.

"What are you frowning about?" she asked.

He took hold of the paint tray as he replied, "You're probably going to need a second coat."

"Maybe. But not today." She stepped back as he descended. When he reached the ground, she took the tray and roller from him.

They stood there in the grass beside the freshly painted barn wall, both of them paint spattered and grinning, just looking at each other. It probably should have felt awkward, even weird, just to stand there and stare at a guy she barely knew.

But it didn't. She liked the look of him, lean and rangy, ready for anything.

He said, "I have fences to check and a ditch or two to clear tomorrow." He took off his hat and raked his hand back through his hair. "Should be able to get away in the early afternoon, though. I'll come by then, help you finish up here."

She blinked in surprise. "Wait—no. You don't have to—"

"I know I don't. But I want to." He seemed sincere. Really, she liked the guy way too much. He was charming and sexy and confident—and yet kind of unassuming at the same time.

Now she was frowning. "What's this all about, Graham Callahan?"

He actually chuckled then, a sound as easygoing and good-natured as the man himself. "I'm that obvious, huh?"

"Well, something's going on, and you need to tell me what."

"I will."

"When?"

"Tomorrow. Soon as we finish putting on that second coat."

"Let me guess. You're doing this because you want me to owe you."

He laughed then, just tossed back his dark head and laughed out loud. The sound was contagious. Suddenly she was laughing, too.

When they both fell silent, he said, "Maybe not *owe* me, exactly. But I wouldn't mind at all if you decided you were willing to do me a really big favor."

She narrowed her eyes at him. "What kind of favor?"

"Tomorrow," he repeated. "Two o'clock." He tipped his hat to her and then settled it more firmly on his head. "See you then."

She watched him jog back across the meadow, boost himself easily over the fence, climb into his long bed crew cab pickup and drive away.

"Was that Graham Callahan I saw helping you paint the barn?" asked Cassie's mom, Olive, as she passed Cassie the potatoes.

"Yep." Cassie served herself and handed the bowl to her brother.

"I got a pretty good look at him when he was getting back into his pickup," said her mom. "He's grown into such a good-looking young man. Don't you think so?"

"Absolutely," Cassie replied flatly, picturing her mom peeking out between the curtains of one of the windows that looked out over the front yard and the meadow beyond it.

"Oh, yes," said Olive in a dreamy tone. "Such a handsome man…"

Cassie said nothing. The whole point right now was to discourage further mention of Graham and his good looks.

Her mom failed to take the hint. "He seemed quite taken with you, honey."

"I don't think so, Mom—and we were across the road and all the way on the far side of the meadow. How could you tell if he was 'taken' with me or not?"

"Well, I could hear you talking and laughing. Sound carries, you know. You both seemed to enjoy chatting with each other. Plus, he did stay for several hours."

"Were you watching us out the front window, Mom?"

"What? I can't glance out my own window now and then? Not that I could see all that much even if I *was* looking. As you mentioned, it's a ways across that meadow..."

"Mom. Let it go."

"I hear he's running for mayor." Olive beamed. "I like a man with a sense of responsibility to the community."

Cassie made a noncommittal sound and concentrated on her dinner as her dad and her brother began discussing the alfalfa crop.

Good, she thought, and hoped the two of them kept right on talking about hay all through the rest of the meal. Olive would have no chance to say more about Graham Callahan.

Lately her mom was driving her right up the wall with all this pressure to *put herself out there again,* to *give love a chance.* Her mom would not back off, even though Cassie had explained in excruciating detail the very real reasons why wedding bells would not be ringing for her.

Olive Trent was a hopeless romantic and way too proud of that fact. She and Cassie's dad had raised four children. And they still adored each other after thirty-five years of marriage. Growing up, the ranch house had been full of kids running up and down the stairs, talking over each other, laughing, crying, fighting and making up.

Nowadays, things were quieter. Only Cassie and Ryder still lived in the main house. Cassie's older brother, Noah, had his own house there on the ranch, a house he shared with his fiancée and his three sons.

Renee had her own place, too. She lived in a cute bungalow, also right there on the ranch. Miles had moved in with her a while back. He commuted to the Parker family ranch most days to work with his brother Hayes and their dad.

Mostly Cassie didn't mind living in her parents' house. But lately, the situation was getting on her last nerve. Her mom honestly believed that a woman's life wasn't complete without a man to adore her and give her three or four precious babies. Olive Trent wanted each and every one of her kids to experience the joy and fulfillment of marital bliss. She was getting what she wanted for both Noah and Renee. Why couldn't that be enough for her?

Down the table, her mom smiled at her way too sweetly. "You should ask Graham to be your date for the wedding."

Cassie stifled a groan. "Mom, please don't—"

"Hear me out. I know, I know. People say Graham Callahan has broken more than one girl's poor heart."

"Mom, there is no point in—"

"Not finished, hon." Her mom blasted her with another sugary smile. "*I* say, Graham Callahan is simply not willing to settle for less than true love, and I say that means when the right woman comes along, he won't hesitate. He'll go all in from the gate. And I have a feeling—a very strong feeling—that the right woman for Graham Callahan just might be you."

Where to even start with that? "I love you, Mom,"

Cassie said through clenched teeth. "I love you, but I think I do need to make something crystal clear to you."

"And what's that, honey?"

"You don't have a clue what you're talking about."

"Wrong. I do."

"You don't, Mom."

"I do. I know what I'm talking about because I'm a woman, too."

"Yeesh!" Cassie slid a glance at her brother. No help there. Ryder was enjoying his Swiss steak and watching the exchange between his mother and sister like it was a tennis match, his head going back and forth with each shot from either side of the argument.

She let her gaze stray to her dad. Same thing. Christopher Trent was staring straight at her now, waiting for her response.

Her mom looked at Cassie with sad eyes. "I just don't understand what has happened to you. You were always the family romantic, remember? You were planning your wedding to Butch Bixby when you were only seventeen..." Star quarterback for the Tenacity Titans, Butch had been Cassie's everything back in the day.

"Seriously, Mom? Do we *have* to go through all that again? Stuff happened. I'm not that dreamy-eyed high school girl anymore. I understand myself better and I know who I really am now—and Mom, I happen to *like* who I really am. I love my life. I'm very happy. There is no problem here. There really isn't."

"It's just a date," her mom said sweetly, coaxingly. "Just one date, that's all."

"Just one date..."

"That is what I said."

"Just one date, and then what?"

"Hmm." Olive seemed thoughtful. And then her mouth bloomed in another beatific smile. "I'll tell you what. If you bring a date to your sister's wedding, I promise to stop pressuring you to find your own true love."

Cassie asked cautiously, "For how long?"

"Excuse me?"

"If I bring a date to the wedding, will you promise never to pressure me about dating again?"

Olive frowned. "Sweetheart. Forever is a long, long time."

"All right, then. If you can't stop matchmaking me for the rest of our lives, how long *can* you stop for?"

Olive actually gave that question serious thought. "Hmm…" She sat up straighter and pulled her shoulders back. "A year." She said it firmly. "Bring a date to the wedding, and for one full year, I won't try to *matchmake* you as you put it, or pressure you to find a nice guy to go out with."

Cassie sat back in her chair. Because that offer was actually tempting. A full year without another conversation like this one at dinnertime. A full year in which her mother didn't once remind her of all the ways she was missing out due to not being madly in love with some dude. "I don't know, Mom. I just don't think you'll be able to keep that deal."

Olive set down her fork. "Cassie Trent. You know me better than that. When I give my word, I keep it." She really did seem to mean it. And even if she broke her promise, Cassie could probably guilt her into backing off.

"One date," Cassie clarified. "For the wedding…"

Her mom laughed and clapped her hands. "Oh, please let it be Graham Callahan. He's such a charmer, and I heard you two laughing together today. I knew then. I told myself, 'Olive. That is the man and this is the moment.'"

"Mom. Pay attention. We're negotiating a deal, and the deal is that I go to the wedding with a man of my choosing and for one full year, you won't matchmake me or push me to find a man to date. Will you make that deal or not?"

Her mom picked up her water glass, raised it high and then drank it down. "Done," she announced, and plunked the empty glass back on the table.

Chapter Three

When Graham showed up the next day, he found Cassie hard at work rolling a second coat of paint on the side of the barn.

She must have heard him drive up. As he pulled to a stop by the meadow fence, she set her roller in the tray and waved at him.

He got out of the pickup and called to her, "Hey! You were supposed to wait for me."

She laughed and shouted, "You snooze, you lose, Callahan." Meanwhile, down at the far end of the meadow, the goats bleated enthusiastically, their noses poked between the wires of their pen.

He jumped the rail fence and jogged straight for her. When he stood by her side, he said, "I see you got the ladder out already."

She handed him a brush and a half-full can of red paint. "You're so good at cutting in. I figured you could just start with that."

"Works for me." He was thinking how great she looked—in that natural, confident, effortless way of hers. She was slim, of medium height, with a full, wide mouth and enormous blue eyes. Today, same as yesterday, she wore her shiny, straight blond hair pulled back in a low ponytail under her straw hat…

And she was looking up at him expectantly—because, yeah, he should probably stop staring. He stuck the paintbrush in a back pocket and turned to climb the ladder.

She caught his bare forearm. It felt way too good—the press of her fingers on his flesh. "Just a minute, big guy."

He paused on the bottom rung. Their eyes met. He felt that zing, the one a man gets when there's real chemistry. "I'm listening."

"You still haven't told me what you need to talk with me about."

"Let's get the job done first."

"But I'm curious."

"Good." He gave her a grin. "So let's finish here and then we can talk." The goats chose that moment to up their game. They ranged along the fence that penned them in, bleating louder than ever. He asked, "Do you need to go find out what the racket's about?"

"Are you kidding? If I ran to check on them every time they made a little noise, I would never get anything else done—which is pretty much their plan. They honestly believe that I should devote my life to hanging out with them."

The shadow of her hat brim ended at her nose and he found himself staring at her soft mouth, thinking that he really wanted to kiss her.

But he wasn't here for kisses—not today, anyway. He needed to finish painting the damn barn and then convince her that she should get on board with his plan. "So, then," he heard himself ask lamely, "shall we get after it?"

About then, she seemed to realize that she still had hold

of his arm. She let go. He tried really hard not to wish she hadn't. "Yeah," she said, her voice just a little bit husky. "Let's finish this job."

Two hours later, he descended the ladder for the last time just as she finished painting down below.

"Looks really good," she declared as they stood back to check for areas that needed more paint. "This job is done."

"It does look great," he agreed. "Come on. I'll help you clean up."

She put up a hand. "Thanks, but I can handle the cleanup myself. Right now I want to know what it is you keep putting off talking to me about."

He frowned. *Had* he been putting it off?

Possibly. He was afraid she would turn him down. After all, there was no reason she should feel obligated to help him out just because he'd insisted on pitching in to paint the side of her barn.

He needed to get it over with and move on. "How 'bout a beer?"

"Sure."

He held out his paint-flecked hand. "Come on then."

She didn't hesitate, just laid her equally paint-spattered fingers in his. He pulled her toward his pickup.

When they reached the rail fence, he released her hand. "Wait right here." He jumped the fence and pulled open the back seat door of his crew cab. Flipping the lid on the cooler he'd stashed back there, he grabbed a pair of ice-cold longnecks. After knocking off the caps, he passed one over the fence to her. The bottles made a cheerful clinking sound as they tapped them together across the top rail.

She took a long sip. "Really hits the spot," she said. "Thank you."

"My pleasure."

Hitching a boot up on the lower rail, she hoisted herself to the top of the fence and sat down. He did the same. They both took a couple more sips before she said, "Okay, Callahan. Whatever it is you keep putting off saying, time's up. Lay it on me."

Where to start? "Well, Cassie, I've been thinking about what you said the other day at the Silver Spur…"

"I said a lot of things that day. You're going to have to be more specific."

He drew a slow, careful breath. "As you pointed out, I have an image problem that could keep me from becoming mayor. And I just can't help thinking that you're the solution to my problem."

"Uh-oh," she said. But at least she was grinning. And her eyes looked even bluer than before.

"Hear me out. Please?"

"I'm listening."

"I need a good woman by my side to make voters trust me."

Cassie laughed outright. "Sorry, Graham. No, I'm not running for city council and I don't want to be deputy mayor."

"I heard you. This isn't about that."

"Then, what…?"

"I want you to date me."

Those big blue eyes got even bigger. "Whoa. Hold on, there, cowboy…"

Damn. Had he messed this up already? He put up a hand. "Don't say no yet. Just listen."

"Really, no. I'm…flattered, I am. But I don't date."

"Okay, now *I'm* confused." And hurt, too. Which was ridiculous. Why should he be hurt that she wouldn't date him? He didn't want to date her, either—he didn't want to date anyone. Not for real. Hadn't he made that clear? "Let me try again. What I meant was—"

"Graham—" she cut him off "—it's not you. I know that's what women always say when they don't want to go out with a guy, but in this case, I swear to you. It's not you. No matter what my mother tells you—or any of the other would-be matchmakers in this town—I'm not interested in getting together with a guy. Not any guy. Not ever again. I. Don't. Date."

Now he was intrigued. "Why not?"

She knocked back a gulp of beer. "Long story."

Was it possible they had even more in common than he'd realized? Hadn't she dated that saddlemaker, Jake McGeorge, a while back? And then Jake had left town, hadn't he?

"I've got time," he said. "Talk to me. Just lay it right out there."

"It's simple. My mother's constantly on my case. She wants me to find the right man and settle down. Lately, she's become nothing short of relentless about it. But I'm not interested in anything remotely resembling a relationship with a guy. That whole love thing? It's just not for me."

He really was curious. "But why?"

"Long story, not telling it."

"What about marriage?"

"What about it?"

"Well, Cassie, someday you're going to want to—"

"No. That's not happening. No true love. No marriage. None of that stuff."

"Wow."

She pointed her beer at him. "You're just like all men. You think every woman you meet is hanging around waiting for some guy to love them? Well, I'm not. I'm done with all that. And as I've told my mother more times than I care to count, I'm happy with my life just the way it is."

And now he *really* wanted to hear her story.

But he could see in those gorgeous blue eyes that she wouldn't be sharing that story today—which was fine. He could wait.

He shifted on the top rail and took another sip of beer. "Okay, let's try it this way…"

She eyed him warily. "Which way?"

"Do you think you might be willing to help me out?"

"With what?"

"See, it's like this. I've been thinking that having you at my side through the campaign could really improve my chances for a win."

"I already explained to you—"

"I know, I know. I get what you said about the deputy mayor thing. It's a no-go and I understand that. But still, you've got a level head on your shoulders and you call it like you see it. I can use your advice. Plus, if you're at my side a lot, people will assume we're a couple, and that will make me look more grounded—you know, less like the player you say everyone thinks I am."

"Graham." She was hiding a smile.

He asked cautiously, "Yeah?"

"Don't be offended, but you actually *are* the player everyone thinks you are."

He felt kind of ashamed. "Yeah, I get that. I'm not interested in settling down—which you ought to understand, given that you just told me you feel the same way."

"Where are you going with this?"

"I'm just saying that neither of us is planning to get married anytime soon."

"Well, I'm not," she declared. "That's for sure."

"Exactly. And as for me, I don't want to get married any more than you do. What I do want is to step up as this town's mayor. But to get elected, I need to change my image."

She bit her pillowy lower lip and shrugged. "Well, yeah. You probably do. People are feeling pretty screwed over after Mayor Woodson's dirty tricks and his wife's bad behavior."

"No kidding," he agreed. "And Marty Moore isn't much of an improvement. This town needs a mayor who inspires confidence and trust. That's why I need a steady girlfriend—to reassure everyone that I've got both feet on solid ground and that I have no intention of breaking any more tender hearts."

"Okay. Let me get this straight. You want to fake date me to make yourself look more dependable."

He winced. "You know, it sounds kind of bad when you put it like that."

She laughed. "You think?"

"Our dates would be actual dates," he suggested hopefully. "And we get along, so you can bet we would have a good time. People are going to think what they want, and we would let them. We don't have to tell them we're just good buddies who enjoy getting together."

She held out her empty bottle. "I'm going to need another one of these."

"You got it." He accepted the empty bottle from her, jumped down off the fence and got two more beers from the back seat. "Here you go." He passed one to her and climbed back up beside her. They both drank at the same time. Then he said, "Look at it this way. It's for a good cause."

She chuckled, the sound more than a little ironic. "I do appreciate the hours you put in painting the barn to butter me up."

"Hold on, now. I was happy to help, I really was. We do get along, you and me. I like to think we might be friends. And as your friend, I'm happy to pitch in whenever you need me."

Now she looked slightly pained. "Sorry. Really, Graham. You're great. You're helpful and you're fun. Easy on the eyes, too."

What was he supposed to say to that? "Thanks?"

"Oh, come on. You can't blame me for having serious doubts about this fake-relationship plan of yours."

"I understand." But that didn't mean he was willing to give up. "So how 'bout you let me help you dispel those doubts?"

She slanted him a sideways look. "Good luck with that."

"Just think about it then. Because, Cassie, I really believe it could work—for both of us. I'll look more stable and solid. And if you want your mother to stop pushing you to date someone, why not let her think you're dating me? Win/win for both of us."

She actually seemed to be giving the idea some thought for a moment. But then she shook her head. "And then what? We date until the election, after which we suddenly break up?"

"I was thinking that we would be seeing each other at least until the election, yeah—and after that, we would decide together how and when to…drift apart."

"Hmm," she said softly.

He asked hopefully, "What are you thinking?"

She tapped the base of her beer bottle on the top rail and then drank some more. "Okay. The truth is, I kind of made a deal with my mom."

He leaned in closer. "What sort of deal?"

"It's like this. If I bring a date to Renee's wedding, my mother won't matchmake me or nag me about finding a man—not for one whole year."

He grinned. Because he knew right then that it was all going to work out. For both of them. "Cassie," he scolded, "why didn't you tell me that right away?"

"I'm not sure. Maybe because I knew that as soon as I told you, I would also agree to go along with your plan."

He suppressed a triumphant smile. "So then. It's perfect. You'll have a date for your sister's wedding with a guy who will never be popping the question. And I'll have a fake girlfriend to make me look serious and stable."

She took off her hat, beat it once on her slim, denim-covered thigh and clamped it back on her head. "You know, it really does sound devious and underhanded."

"No, no, no," he said softly. "It's practical, it works for both of us and no one gets hurt. Plus, come on. We have a great time together. We get along. Seriously. Think about it. It's going to be fun."

She shot him a doubtful look. "Strictly for show, though, right?"

He put up his hand, palm out. "I solemnly swear I won't put a move on you."

She met his eyes directly. "You know what? I believe you. And I would love to get my mom to back off. But I'm still uncomfortable with it. I mean, beginning your campaign for mayor with a fake relationship isn't the best way to go about winning the community's trust."

"It's a white lie." He kept his voice steady and low. "It's reassuring to the community, and nobody gets hurt."

"I just don't know, Graham…" She was frowning at him.

Was he pushing too hard? "Look. Thanks for hearing me out. Just…please think about it?"

Slowly she nodded. Then she handed him her empty beer bottle and pulled her phone from the back pocket of her Wranglers. "Give me your number."

He rattled off the digits and she added him to her contacts. "Call me," he said, and jumped down from the fence. "Let me know what you decide." She looked down at him, her expression unreadable. He was suddenly sure she would end up rejecting his plan.

But what could he do? He'd already pushed her more than he should have. Turning, he opened the back seat door, put the empties in the cooler and pushed the door shut.

He was just about to climb in behind the wheel when she jumped to the ground on his side of the fence. He heard her boots hit the dirt and he turned her way again.

"Okay, Graham," she said. "My sister's wedding is Saturday, the twenty-third. If you can be my date for that, I'm in."

It was a good moment, the two of them standing there at the fence, grinning at each other. At the far end of the meadow, her goats set up a ruckus again. "Maa… Maa… Maa…"

He realized he was actually looking forward to being Cassie Trent's fake boyfriend. "Count me in for the wedding."

She nodded. "All right, then. We have a plan."

"You ready to get started?"

Her gaze didn't waver. "No time like the present."

"Tomorrow night, then. Six o'clock. I'll take you to the Tenacity Social Club."

She made a low, thoughtful sound. "That'll get people talking."

He could hardly believe that she'd actually agreed to go through with it. "So you really are in this?"

"You bet I am. I'll meet you there. Tomorrow. Six o'clock. Don't you dare keep me waiting, Graham."

"I won't. See you then."

"What's going on in here?"

Cassie glanced up from the various articles of clothing strewn across her bed to see Renee leaning in the doorway to the upstairs hall. Buddy, Renee's service dog, sat panting happily at her feet. Renee had Type 1 diabetes, and the sweet-natured yellow Labrador retriever was trained to detect any dangerous changes in her blood sugar levels.

"Hey—" Cassie waved Renee over "—I need advice."

With Buddy trailing in her wake, Renee approached the bed. "Advice about…?"

Cassie hardly knew where to begin—let alone how much to say. "You're not going to believe this."

"Hit me with it."

"I have a date tonight. I'm meeting Graham Callahan at the Tenacity Social Club."

"A date?" Renee blinked in sheer disbelief. "You're kidding."

"Nope. Dead serious."

"But Cassie. You don't date."

"Yeah, well…" Cassie considered how much to say. She trusted her sister with her life and all her secrets. But why go there? Renee didn't really need to know. Not to mention that, at this point anyway, there was no reason to ask Renee to take on the burden of hiding the truth from their mom. "What can I say? I like him." Hey, it was true. She did like Graham. "He's a charmer and one date never hurt anybody. As for the future, we'll see how it goes."

Renee offered carefully, "They say he'll never settle down." And then she grinned. "And you say you won't, either."

Cassie nodded. "That's right. See? Graham and I have something in common."

Renee stroked Buddy's broad head. The dog wagged his tail and gave a happy little whine. "Mom mentioned that Graham came by and helped you repaint the side of the barn."

"Of course, Mom did."

"Does she know you're going out with him?"

"Let me put it this way, if she doesn't know already, she'll find out soon enough—and right now, I need to decide what to wear."

Rene was grinning again. "The Social Club, you said?"

"That's right."

Renee surveyed the options Cassie had laid out on the bed. "The white off-the-shoulder knit top. And this." Renee held up a high-low button front skirt with a ruffled hem. "And your Tecovas with the turquoise tooling on the shaft."

"Hmm. I like it."

They beamed at each other. "You're welcome," said Renee.

In the basement of the building that also housed the post office and barber shop, the Tenacity Social Club had started out as a speakeasy a hundred years ago. Now it was a popular gathering place for various community activities and events, the kind of spot you might bring a first date if you wanted to signal that it was more than a hookup.

That night, Cassie entered the underground club at six on the dot. It was a special place, really. During the day, the space was used as a hangout for local teenagers—it was an alcohol-free zone till five at night. After that, the Social Club operated as a bar. There was an old-school pinball machine, a jukebox and a dance floor. On the weekends, local musicians played there. But, if you studied the flyers on the wall, they advertised things like math tutoring and glee club.

Tonight, there were quite a few locals in the place, more than usual for a Wednesday night. The jukebox was playing a Luke Combs song and a small group of people two-stepped on the dance floor.

Cassie spotted Graham right away. He stood at the bar facing the door, waiting for her. She smiled at him. His slow grin had her thinking, *This guy is dangerous.* But that didn't stop her from weaving her way to him—because of the election, she reminded herself staunchly. And because she needed a date for the wedding, a date that would get her mom off her case for one full year.

So what if she had a slightly swoopy sensation low in her belly when he grinned at her? It was called *chemistry* and chemistry was good. Chemistry would make it more likely that folks in town would see their make-believe romance as the real deal.

People were watching. Cassie pretended not to notice. She waved and called greetings to people she knew as she passed them. When she reached Graham's side at the bar, he leaned close enough that she could smell his fresh, outdoorsy aftershave.

His warm breath brushed her cheek as he whispered, "You look amazing."

"You're not half-bad yourself," she replied, moving back a step to take in his crisp yoked shirt and dress jeans.

"Bare shoulders," he remarked. "Dangerous..."

"How so?"

He shook his head. "I'm thinking I'd better not go there."

She tugged on the point of his collar. "Good answer."

He pulled out the empty stool next to him. As she took the seat, she admired the bar, which was an old wooden plank carved with many years' worth of lovers' initials. Cassie's mom always said that bar read like a who's who of Tenacity.

Graham signaled Mike Cooper, the bartender.

"Cassie Trent." Mike greeted her with a warm smile. "What can I get you?"

She ordered a mojito, and Graham asked for whiskey on the rocks. When Mike set the drinks down, Graham offered a toast. "To true love forever."

She scoffed. "Seriously?"

He just waited, his glass raised high, until she tapped her mojito against it. They drank, neither of them breaking eye contact. It felt...real. Too real.

She was having a great time playing at falling for the man beside her, even if a little voice in the back of her head kept warning, *Watch it. Don't go too far. It's just a game. This isn't real...*

When she set her glass down, Mike leaned on the bar and asked, "How long have you two been seeing each other?"

"This is our first date," Cassie replied.

"Finally," added Graham, with a totally convincing look of mild exasperation. "I've been trying to get this woman to go out with me for the longest time." He sounded so sincere. If she hadn't known the truth, Cassie would have bought that lie hook, line and sinker. And he wasn't finished. He stared right at her till she met those flirty dark eyes. Then he added, "I'm hoping this is the start of something big."

She let out an absurd little squeak of laughter—because she just couldn't help herself. He was laying it on pretty thick and it was working. The man was so dang charming, Cassie could almost forget that this was all make-believe. "Don't get ahead of yourself," she advised in a teasing tone. "It *is* our first date, after all."

"You mean there's no hope?" He clapped his hand to his heart. "You're killing me here, Cassie."

Was her face red? It sure felt like it. "I'm just saying that falling for someone takes time." She looked in his eyes and willed him to bring it down a notch. "It's not like it happens instantly."

"Sorry, Cassie," Mike cut in. "But I've got to disagree with you on that point. You never know. Yeah, for some, love can take years to grow. But then sometimes, no matter how hard you fight it, you know it's the real thing from the very first moment…" Now Mike had a starry-eyed look on his face. "What I'm trying to say is, when it's right, it's right."

Sheesh. Between Graham and Mike, you'd think life was one long lovefest. She knew that Graham was just playing his role here. Not Mike, though. Several months ago, Mike had gotten together with wealthy cattle rancher

Daniel Taylor. Now the two of them were deeply in love and planning a life together.

No, she shouldn't rain on the bartender's parade. But her more cynical side refused to let it go. "Love might have been a thunderbolt for you, Mike. But for most people it does take time." *And for some of us, it never really happens at all.*

A frown creased Mike's brow. "Hold on. I never said it was *easy*. I said when it happens, you know it deep down, even if you fight it, even if you tell yourself it's not real. But then, at some point you see that there's no denying what you feel in your heart. And you look back and you realize that there was something there right from the first—that you *knew* right out of the gate that this was it..." He blinked and then seemed a bit sheepish as he shoveled ice, whiskey and lemon juice into a shaker. "Truth is," he added with a wry smile, "I wish my sister could find someone special."

Graham asked, "How's Maggie doing?"

"Well enough, I guess..."

Cassie said, "She's been back in town for how long now?"

"A few months." Mike put the lid on the shaker. Ice rattled cheerfully as he shook it. "Things aren't easy for her. Maggie could use a strong shoulder to lean on—I mean, other than mine." He poured the drink into a glass, garnished it and got to work on a matched pair of whiskey sours. "The thing is, I'm afraid it's never going to happen for Maggie. She's had a hard time and she's reluctant to give her trust again."

The server stepped up to the bar and tapped the side of the tray of drinks Mike had just finished mixing. "Is this ready?"

He nodded. "Yep."

"Great." She picked up the tray and headed for the tables.

Mike grabbed a bar towel and wiped up a spill. When he glanced up at Cassie again, he said, "And about Maggie. If you think of a good guy who might be right for her..."

"I will reach out to you," Cassie promised. "But Mike, you probably know everyone in town better than I do."

Mike shrugged. "Maybe so." At the far end of the bar, a cowboy signaled for another round. Mike headed on down there.

"Hey," said Graham, leaning her way and nudging her shoulder with his.

"What now?" She laughed as she nudged him right back.

He moved in even closer and whispered, "If I were to put my arm around you, would you consider that too bold a move for a first date?"

She looked directly at him and couldn't help thinking, *No wonder all those girls lost their poor hearts to this guy.* "You are enjoying this far too much," she teased.

He arched a dark eyebrow. "So, then. Yes, I should go ahead and put my arm around you?"

She slid a quick glance over her shoulder and spotted several familiar faces. One or two of those people just might have been paying attention to what was going on at the bar between her and Graham.

And that was the point, after all, for the whole town to see the beginnings of a beautiful romance.

Again, she leaned close to him. "Yes," she said. "Put your arm around me. Now."

The look in his eyes changed. One minute they twinkled with teasing good humor. The next, they were focused. Sizzling hot.

"Do it," she muttered under her breath. It came out sounding like she was asking for something deliciously bad.

He made his move then, sliding his arm around her and easing his warm, rough fingers up under hair. His thumb brushed the vulnerable skin at the nape of her neck. "Like this?" His thumb kept brushing back and forth. It felt good—too good.

She should probably tell him to lower the heat level. But then again, no way. "Callahan, you're far too much fun, you know that?"

"And guess what? I'm just getting started."

Cassie picked up her mojito and gulped down a big icy sip to cool herself off a bit. "Most men aren't so..."

"What?"

"I don't know. Playful, I guess. In my experience, men are focused and serious, and they wear you out with their plans and their ambitions and their goals that they view as so much more important than anything a woman might want for her own life."

He pulled back from her a little, his expression serious now. But then he leaned close again to whisper, "So that's why you've sworn off love and romance?"

"Partly, yeah." The song on the jukebox changed to something sweet and slow. "But it's not only that. I like my life as a single woman and I'm not giving it up."

He watched her so closely. "I get it. I do."

"Well, good, then." She raised her mojito. "To the single life."

He tapped his glass to hers. "Dance with me."

"I would love to." She set her fingers in his, and they

wove through the tables to the dance floor, where two other couples swayed to the music. He pulled her close—but not too close. The way he held her was just right for a first dance.

Miranda Lambert and Leon Bridges crooned "If You Were Mine"—which she wasn't and he wasn't and neither would ever be. But still, the song was made for that moment, for the two of them who would never be each other's everything—and yet, if that were possible, well, hey… A girl can dream.

They swayed together. He was a good dancer, easy to follow, not trying to get too fancy. She felt eager, wound up. The dim basement bar seemed to glow with promise. Like they were at the beginning of a big adventure—and maybe they were. Two people who had sworn off love, faking a magical first date for all they were worth.

When the next song began, neither of them said a word. They kept on dancing. It happened again with the song after that. There were fast ones—"Here for the Party," "She Thinks my Tractor's Sexy" and "Suds in the Bucket" to name just a few.

Several dances later, they paused, shared a look and a nod—and headed back to the bar.

"Another round?" asked Mike.

"I should go…" she said, but didn't really want to.

Graham suggested, "Just one more?"

"Yes," she said with absolutely no hesitation.

Chapter Four

At a little after nine, they said good-night to Mike and climbed the stairs to street level.

Graham didn't really want to leave. Cassie Trent was something special—not only fun and easy on the eyes, but thoughtful, too. He'd had a great time just sitting at the bar with her. She was honestly interested in other people, in what they had to say and what was going on in their lives.

And when he'd taken her in his arms for that first dance together, he'd realized that the chemistry between them might be a problem—if he didn't watch himself.

But then again, he wasn't some green kid with a first crush. He would keep a tight rein on himself in private and all would be well. In public, though? Well, that was a whole other story.

There would be PDAs. After all, they needed everyone in town to believe that they really were a couple. That meant he would be kissing Cassie in public. He shouldn't be so eager to get going on that.

So shoot him. He couldn't wait.

When they reached street level and went out the door between the post office and the barbershop, the day was fading fast, twilight settling like a soft blanket over Central Avenue. The air had cooled quickly as the sun faded.

It was nice out, in the low seventies now. By unspoken agreement, they just started walking along the sidewalk in the fading twilight, ending up at Tenacity's lone bus stop, where they sat on the single bench side by side.

Across the street, the door to their town's other night-spot, the Grizzly Bar, was wide-open. He could hear people laughing, music playing, the faint sounds of pool balls clacking together.

"I should get going," she said, but made no move to leave. Instead, she turned to him. Her big eyes were shad-owed in the growing darkness. "So, Callahan. How'd we do?"

"Bam!" He put on his most confident grin. "Out of the park. Grand slam, no doubt about it."

She was nodding. "You know, I kind of thought so, too. It was a really good start."

He considered kissing her right now. But no. Probably too soon for that—not to mention there was no one to see him do it. "So then, what's next?"

She tipped her head down and looked up at him from under her lashes. "Hey, you're the man with the plan. I'm just your fake girlfriend."

"Don't underestimate yourself." He was careful to speak quietly, in case someone wandered by. "Not only are you the best fake girlfriend I've ever had, hands down—"

"Wait a minute. There have been others?"

"Hell, no. I don't fool around when it comes to fake girlfriends—so yeah, that makes you my *only* fake girl-friend. But even though you're my first, I already know that no one else will ever compare."

She groaned. "You're over-the-top, you know that?"

"Maybe. A little—and by the way, I've decided to tell everyone that you're my campaign manager."

Cassie laughed. "What is it with you, always trying to give me some official title? Deputy mayor, campaign manager…"

"Yeah, but in this case you don't really have to do anything except go out with me."

"I'm already on board with that. I don't need a title, truly I don't."

But he wanted to give her one. He wanted to find more reasons than just fake dating to be with her whenever possible.

And why, exactly, did he want to be around her so much?

He decided not to think about that. Overthinking, after all, was never a good idea.

He put his arm around her and felt downright thrilled when she let him do it, even though the chances of them being observed at this moment were pretty low. "Look at it this way…" He had to actively resist the urge to nuzzle her hair. She smelled delicious, but nuzzling would probably be over the line—and what was he about to say, anyway? It took him a second or two to remember. "I'll call you my campaign manager, but it will be like when men call their wives their 'better half.' Everyone will know it's just me saying how important you are to me."

She snickered. "How do you manage to come up with this stuff?"

He put on a somber expression. "I take this campaign very seriously." He could sit here like this all night, kidding around with her, his arm slung across her shoulders.

"Graham…"

"Hmm?"

She shifted slightly. He took the hint and reluctantly let

go of her. Then she reminded him, "We do have to decide what's next in this fake relationship of ours."

"Simple. We need to spend time together."

"In public, right?"

He thought about that and realized he didn't really give a damn if they were seen together or not. He just wanted to hang around with her—which troubled him for a second or two. Because he and Cassie were supposed to be just for show.

But then he reminded himself that he really did like her. Why shouldn't he want to hang out with her whenever he got the chance? It wasn't a romantic thing. She was good people and they got along.

However, they did have a goal, and the goal was to convince the citizens of Tenacity that he wasn't some wild skirt chaser, that he was a guy who could settle down with one special woman—a dependable guy, the kind of guy people could trust with their vote.

So he agreed, "Yeah. We should focus on getting out in public together. You available Friday night?"

"Sure."

"Castillo's?" The little Mexican restaurant was also right there on Central Avenue. "I'll pick you up at seven."

"I can meet you there, Graham."

"No way. It's our second date. What will people think if you don't trust me enough to ride in my pickup after our beautiful night at the Social Club?"

Widening her eyes and pressing her hand to her heart, she pretended to balk. "I'm not sure about this. You seem kind of dangerous." They grinned at each other.

"I promise, I'm harmless." He stood. "And I am picking you up at seven on Friday—now, come on. I'll walk you to your truck."

* * *

The next day, Cassie had just finished the morning milking and stored the milk in the minifridge she kept in the shed not far from the goat pen, when she heard a vehicle drive up.

She left the shed, rounded the pen and spotted Vicky's little SUV as it stopped in front of the main house. Vicky got out and headed for the porch steps.

It was early, not even eight in the morning yet—maybe a little too early for her best friend to show up out of the blue. Was something wrong?

Cassie took off at jog for the meadow gate. "Vicky!" she called, waving as she ran.

Vicky turned from the front steps and raised an arm in response. Cassie hurried across the two-track road and went through the low front gate to meet her at the foot of the steps.

"Everything okay?" Cassie asked.

"Yeah. Fine."

"You sure?"

Vicky frowned. "Yeah. I'm all right, really. I know I'm kind of early. But I was thinking about you and decided I'd just drop by, see how you're doing. Is this a bad time?"

"Are you kidding? I'm always glad to see you." They shared a hug. "How about some coffee?"

"Yes, please."

Inside, Cassie led the way to the kitchen. "Have a seat."

"Where is everyone?" Vicky sat down at the table.

"Out working." Cassie loaded up the coffee maker. Through the window over the sink, she could see her mom puttering around in her garden. "Mom's out back, and I believe Ryder and my dad are busy in the tractor shed changing spark plugs and just possibly replacing a fan belt."

"So...they already had breakfast?"

"That was hours ago."

"Ranch life." Vicky sighed. "To me, it always sounds exhausting."

"Hey, I wouldn't have it any other way."

"I know, I know. But I'll stick with a nice job in town, if you don't mind..." Vicky worked at the little consignment shop not from her small apartment over the grocery store.

"Are you hungry? How about some toast? And I'm more than happy to scramble you some eggs."

"Toast would be perfect."

A few minutes later, Cassie poured their coffee. "So how's your mom?"

Vicky's glum shrug said it all. She spread homemade blackberry jam on her toast. "As I told you Friday, she filed the divorce papers, so it's really happening." She took a bite of toast. "This jam is the best. Tell your mom I love it."

"I will." Cassie waited. Vicky was staring off into the middle distance. "Vick..."

"Hmm?"

"If you're worried about your dad—"

"Are you kidding? My dad can more than take care of himself. Uh-uh. I'm here to talk about rumors and how quickly they spread."

"Rumors about what?"

"Well, I got a call from Larinda Peach an hour ago. We are talking seven in the morning."

"What did she want?"

"What do you think? To gossip. She'd heard that my mom filed for divorce."

"Ugh."

"Exactly. Larinda wanted to know how I was doing. You know how she gets, asking if I was *devastated* in that tone that says, 'Dish me all your dirt so I can turn around and tell everybody in town.'"

"Larinda desperately needs to get a life."

"Tell me about it." Vicky sipped her coffee. "Anyway, I said I was fine and that my mom is doing well—and you know what Larinda did then? She argued with me. She claimed she could tell by my voice that I was on the verge of tears and I should just go ahead and let it all out, that she was there for me."

Cassie put her hand on her friend's arm and gave a reassuring squeeze. "I'm sorry you had to listen to that."

"Yeah. Me, too."

"If she made you cry, I'm going to have to have a long talk with her on the subject of minding her own damn business."

Vicky straightened her spine. "Larinda did not make me cry. She's really not a bad person."

"You're right. She just never takes a hint."

"Exactly."

Cassie said, "But she did back off eventually, right?"

"Not really. She just…moved on."

"To what?"

Vicky made a low, angry sound in her throat. "She started babbling away about you and Graham Callahan meeting up at the Social Club last night."

"Oh," Cassie said sheepishly. "That…"

"Yeah. That." Vicky looked at her accusingly. "You and Graham? Really? And you never said a word to me?"

"I was planning to tell you all about it…"

"When?"

"Soon. I mean, the thing with Graham only started last Friday after you left the Silver Spur."

"Larinda said you two were all over each other last night."

"Oh, please. Consider the source—and come to think of it, Larinda wasn't even there last night. Whoever told her the story got it wrong."

Vicky picked up her mug—and then set it down without taking a sip. "Cassie, what's going on?"

Where to start? "Well, I…"

"Just tell me. Just bring me up to speed."

"Honestly, Vick. We had a lot of fun last night, Graham and me. We danced. But we were hardly all over each other. That's just Larinda stirring the pot—and I really was going to tell you all about the situation with Graham as soon as I got a chance."

"The *situation*? Suddenly you're in a *situation* with Graham Callahan, and I never heard a word about it?"

"Settle down. It's not that big of a deal. As I said, I was planning to tell you, but I had no idea that Larinda would be on the case first thing this morning." Cassie waved a dismissing hand. "This town. News travels faster than a rat up a drainpipe."

Vicky laughed then. "Ew. Some of the things you say…"

Cassie teased, "Sorry. Didn't mean to offend your town-girl sensibilities. Here on the ranch we call it like we see it." She got up to top off their coffee mugs. When she sat back down, she said, "So here's the thing about Graham…"

"Everything, Cassie. I mean it."

"Of course. But you absolutely cannot tell another soul."

"You know me. I am a vault."

"Okay, then. Graham and I are kind of helping each other."

"How?"

"You remember my outdoor-movie idea?"

"I do." Vicky made a sad face. "Sorry it didn't work out."

"Me, too. Anyway, Monday, I finally got started repainting the side of the barn that I was going to use for my movie screen. I was rolling on the red paint when Graham showed up. He pitched right in to help me get the job done."

Vicky offered cautiously, "That was nice of him."

"He had a proposition for me—and no, not the sexy kind. Graham had a plan for how he and I could help each other out."

"Uh-oh," said Vicky.

"Oh, come on. You haven't even heard the story yet."

"Yeah, and already I don't like where you're going with this," Vicky grumbled. "But please. Continue."

Keeping her voice low in case her mom popped in unannounced, Cassie explained that she would be Graham's fake steady girlfriend until the election.

"Why?" asked Vicky, her nose scrunched up like she'd smelled something bad.

"Well, to help him look more dependable, more like the kind of man the citizens of Tenacity would trust to be their mayor."

"I see," Vicky said. Her eyes said something completely different, something more along the lines of, *Have you lost your mind?*

"Vicky, don't judge."

"Just tell me what he's doing to help *you* out."

Cassie glanced over her shoulder to be certain her mom wasn't lurking somewhere nearby. And then she whispered, "While he gets to look more dependable, I get my mom off my back."

"How so?"

Cassie explained about the deal with her mom and how Graham would be her date for the wedding.

When she was finished laying the whole thing out, Vicky said, "Are you sure about this?"

"Yes! Well, I mean, pretty much…"

"You don't sound all that sure."

"Well, I *was* sure. But now I'm looking at you, and you don't look sure at all. Frankly, it's discouraging."

Vicky had another bite of toast. She chewed thoughtfully.

Cassie demanded, "Whatever's going through that mind of yours, just go ahead and say it."

Vicky swallowed, dabbed the corner of her mouth with her napkin and took another sip of coffee. When she finally set down the mug, she said, "I think you like him."

Cassie rolled her eyes so hard, she probably should have tumbled over backward in her chair. "Please. Of course, I like Graham. I would never agree to fake-date a man I didn't like."

Vicky had the nerve to laugh. And then she said, "You know very well what I mean. You *like* him. You've got a thing for him."

Cassie let out a groan of pure exasperation. "You don't know what you're talking about. Yes, I like Graham. I do. But I don't *like* like him. And I certainly do not have a *thing* for him."

"Okay." Vicky smiled sweetly. "If you say so."

"I mean, you know about me. You know *everything*. You know that I am never *like* liking any man ever again."

"Yes. Yes, I know that."

"Well, you don't look like you know it."

"Hey." Vicky put up both hands. "I'm on your side. You know that I am."

Cassie did know. Vicky was her closest friend and that would never change. "Okay, fine. I know you only mean the best for me, and you tell me the truth as you see it."

"You'd better believe I do—because you're my friend forever and I will never tell you anything less than the truth."

"I know."

"Just…be careful, Cass. Please." Now Vicky looked worried.

"Vick, Graham is a good guy. He's not anything like your dad, I promise you. It's all going to be fine."

"This is not about my dad."

"I know, but—"

"Let me finish. Please." Vicky waited until Cassie gave her a nod. Then she said, "Look, I know that I've got a problem, that I don't trust men. How could I? My dad is, and always has been, a nightmare. Still, I am aware that when I look at a guy—just about any guy—I just can't help waiting for whatever dirty trick that guy is going to pull. That's not healthy. Objectively, I understand that all men are not my dad. But still, Graham does have a reputation as a heartbreaker. That's why I can't help thinking that he's just using you."

"He's not."

Vicky groaned. "You can't be sure of that."

"Oh, yes, I can. Because I'm immune to heartbreak, and you ought to know that by now."

Vicky hung her head. "We're all immune—until we're not."

"I know my own heart."

"Ugh. If you say so…"

Cassie sat back with a heavy sigh. "Let me just tell it like it is, okay?"

"Please do."

"Vick, we're using each other, Graham and me. And there doesn't have to be anything wrong with that. Graham's a bit extra, yeah. But at the core, he's a good guy. I really do believe he would make a good mayor. I *know* he's sincere. He wants to do what he can for the good of our town. And I like getting together with him. We have a great time. I'm happy to help him clean up his image, while he helps me get my mom off my case."

Vicky pushed her empty plate away. "I just don't want you to get hurt."

"I won't. I promise you."

Vicky was silent—not that she needed to say a word. Concern and disapproval were written all over her face.

Chapter Five

Graham pulled up in front of the main house on Star-gazer Ranch at seven on the dot Friday evening. He'd barely gotten his door open and his boots on solid ground before Cassie burst out the front door and raced down the steps toward him.

It might be a fake romance between the two of them, but damn! Cassie Trent was downright fine. She wore a short denim skirt and fancy tooled boots, and her shapely, toned legs went on forever. He was going to have to keep a tight rein on himself or he just might start thinking dangerous thoughts.

A big bouquet of sunflowers in his hand, he started around the front of pickup. "You are a sight for sore eyes…"

Now she was frowning. "You brought flowers. You didn't have to do that."

"I thought your mom might—"

"Look." She stopped right in front of him—almost like she was blocking his way. "Let's just go, okay?"

"What? Why?" He swept off his hat and shook his head. "What will your mom think if I don't come inside and say hi like a respectable boyfriend.?"

She leaned up and whispered, "Frankly, I don't care

what my mom thinks." She grabbed his arm. "Now, come on. Let's just—"

He didn't budge. "Cassie."

She let go of him and sighed. "What?"

"If we're doing this, we are doing it right."

She folded her arms. They shared a little stare-down. He knew he'd won when she let her arms drop to her sides. "Fine. Come on in and meet the folks."

He took her slim hand and wove their fingers together. Her palm was slightly rough from ranch work, but not as rough as his own. "Lead the way."

They were halfway up the steps when he saw the curtain on the left side of the door move. A moment later, that door swung wide.

Cassie's mom stood there, beaming. "Graham Callahan, how *are* you?"

"Just great, Mrs.—"

"Oh, no you don't. It's Olive to you."

"Olive." He held out the flowers. "For you."

"Sunflowers!" She took them. "My favorite. How did you know?" She didn't wait for his answer but stepped back and gestured them inside. "Come in, come in."

"Mom," Cassie said. "We really have to—"

"This will only take a minute, sweetheart," Olive cut in sternly. "I'm sure Graham would like to say hello to your dad."

"Of course I would," said Graham, with a quick nod for Cassie—who sent him a mutinous scowl in return. Sweet heaven, she was cute. And he was having a really good time.

"Graham Callahan." Christopher Trent entered the foyer area, hand outstretched. "Come in, come in."

Olive said, "I'll just put these in water and come right back to join you."

Graham exchanged greetings with Mr. Trent. Then they moved into the living room. The three of them had just settled around the big coffee table when Olive reappeared. She sat beside her husband.

Then came the chitchat—the uncomfortable kind that consisted of the older couple asking questions about Graham's siblings and Graham replying in the most generalized, boring way possible. Beside him, Cassie seemed to vibrate with longing to be out the door and gone.

When it finally got to the point where she couldn't take it anymore, she jumped up. "We have to get going," she announced. He started to say that there was no hurry, but she didn't give him the chance. "I mean, we have reservations at Castillo's, right?" She looked at him with her jaw set, determined, come hell or high water, to get them out of there *now*.

He relented. "Yeah, I suppose we ought to be on our way."

The Trent parents followed them to the door. There was more hand-shaking.

Cassie's mom exclaimed, "You two have a wonderful time!"

"We will," he promised.

And then Cassie was pulling him down the front steps. She tried to beat him to the passenger door, but he deftly slipped around her and opened it for her.

"Thank you," she said, turning back to Graham with a big fake smile as she stepped up to the seat.

"My pleasure." He gently shut the door.

With a last wave for her parents, who waved back enthusiastically from up on the porch, he went around and got behind the wheel.

Cassie waited till they were halfway to town before she grumbled, "You really didn't have to go in, you know."

"Sure I did." He sent her a grin. "Let it go."

But she wasn't ready to do that yet. "I want to get my mom off my back, but it's a fine line. There's no need to actively encourage her. If you let her take control, before you know it she'll be planning our wedding."

"Sorry," he said cheerfully.

"No, you're not."

He realized she was right. "Look. Your parents are nice. And hey, back in high school, I always used to like the meet-the-parents stuff."

A frown creased her smooth brow. "I don't believe it. A guy who actually liked getting the third degree before he could hustle his date out the door?"

He stared off toward the mountains in the distance up ahead. "I've always been pretty social. I like getting to know people."

She turned to meet his eyes. "Wait a minute. You said you *used* to enjoy meeting a girl's folks…"

"Right. That was before I decided I was done with all that." He was focused on the road ahead again, but he could feel her watching him.

She said, "I'm growing more and more curious…"

"About?"

"What made you decide you were done with all that?"

"Hey. One of these days…"

"One of these days what, Graham?"

He winked at her. "I'll tell you my sad story, and you can tell me yours."

She made a low, thoughtful sound. "You might be surprised at mine."

"Why?"

"Let me put it this way. Some people just aren't cut out for love and forever after. I'm one of those."

"Got your heart broke bad, huh?"

She shook a finger at him. "Don't push me."

He slanted her a quick, teasing glance. "Was that a dare?"

She laughed. The sound was infectious. He found himself chuckling along with her. And then she taunted, "You first."

"Watch out. I'll do it—and then you'll have to tell me yours."

She slowly shook her head. "Not tonight, that's for sure."

"It's all right. I can wait." He swung the pickup onto Central Avenue and into the small lot behind Castillo's.

Cassie loved Castillo's—but then, so did almost everyone in town. The Castillo family was always welcoming and the food couldn't be beat.

Yolanda Castillo, the family matriarch, greeted them at the door and led them to a booth midway between the entrance and the small bar in back. She rattled off the specials and gave them menus.

"Drinks?" she asked. They ordered Mexican Mules—a tequila version of the Moscow Mule. "Good choice," declared Yolanda. She leaned a little closer and asked Graham, "So then, the campaign is going well?"

"It is," he replied. "It was so good to talk with you and Pablo yesterday." He said to Cassie, "I came by the restaurant with flyers, just to touch base about my plans and the progress of the campaign."

"Ah." Cassie nodded.

"Graham has good ideas for this town," Yolanda decreed and then turned to Graham again. "I put up your flyer on the bulletin board out in front."

"I appreciate that." He caught Cassie's eye. "Cassie here is my—" he let his voice trail off in a teasing way before finishing "—campaign manager." Cassie did her best not to snicker at that one. Yeah, okay, he'd warned her he would call her that, but still, she hadn't really expected him to follow through.

"Hmm," said Yolanda, glancing from him to Cassie and back to Graham again. "You two do seem very…how to say it? Cozy. You two are very cozy."

"We are," Graham declared, reaching out a hand across the table. Cassie played her part and took it.

Cassie said, "Graham and I have discovered that we have a whole lot in common." And they did, given that they'd both sworn off relationships—real ones, anyway.

Yolanda beamed in approval. "It is so beautiful when two young people find each other."

Across the table, Graham stared at Cassie adoringly. She made googly eyes right back at him for all she was worth. About then, one of Yolanda's nieces called to her.

Yolanda raised a hand to show she'd heard and then said that her son, Roberto, would be there to take care of them in a few minutes. With that, she bustled away.

"How'd we do?" whispered Cassie.

"We were amazing," he replied, because he was Graham Callahan and therefore never lacked for enthusiasm—or self-confidence, for that matter.

A couple of minutes later, Roberto appeared with

glasses of ice water, chips and salsa, and their cocktails, too. They both knew what they wanted, so he took their orders.

The food was great, the Mexican Mules cold and delicious. Cassie and her fake boyfriend joked and laughed together. Aside from tonight and Wednesday night at the Social Club, she hadn't been out on a date in forever—not since about three years ago, when she'd called things off with Jake.

Had she ever had this much fun with Jake?

As soon as she asked herself the question, she felt guilty. Jake had been sweet and sincere and serious. She'd tried to be gentle with his tender heart. Too bad she'd failed miserably.

"Hey." Graham was watching her.

"Hmm?"

"What happened? Suddenly you look so sad."

Before she could decide how to answer him, she spotted Marty Moore over Graham's shoulder. Marty was sitting back at the bar. He was staring right at her. She met his shifty eyes, and he wiggled his grizzled white eyebrows in response.

"What is it?" Graham asked. He actually looked a little concerned. "Tell me."

She forced a cool smile and said flatly, "Marty's here."

Graham leaned in. "Sitting at the bar?"

"That's right." She canted toward him good and close. Keeping her voice very low, she added, "Don't give him the satisfaction of turning to look."

"What's he doing?"

"Nothing. Really. He's just…being Marty. But there's something about him, you know? I always feel like he's up to no good. I don't like him and I never have."

Graham reached across the table and put his hand over hers. His touch was warm. Reassuring. "Ignore him."

She nodded. "Done."

They stayed for a second round of Mexican Mules. It really was fun. People stopped by their table to discuss the mayor's race and ask about the upcoming mayoral debate, which was less than three weeks away now. All the candidates had signed up for it, including Graham. As far as Cassie knew, two others besides Graham and Marty were running for mayor—rancher Ellis Corey and stay-at-home mom, Jennilynn Garrett.

Graham told just about everyone they talked to that Cassie was helping him prepare for the debate. That was news to her. But hey. If he needed her help, she would do her best.

"Cassie here is my campaign manager," he explained more than once.

Cassie nodded and said she just wanted to support the campaign in any way she could. She also flirted with him shamelessly—both when people stopped by *and* when they were alone at the table. Because flirting with Graham made people believe their relationship was the real thing. Not to mention, it was a whole lot of fun.

On the way out the door, Yolanda appeared and gave each of them a hug. When she wrapped her soft arms around Cassie, she whispered, "You two come back again soon. Young love is beautiful. It makes everyone happy, and that is good for business."

"We will definitely be back," she promised. At the same time, she couldn't help thinking that their fake romance was moving along awfully fast.

Outside, the August night was warm, the sky overhead

awash in stars. Graham took her hand. She gave him a smile and twined her fingers with his.

The doors to the Grizzly Bar were wide-open as usual. She could hear the juke box playing an old Willie Nelson song. They started walking. It felt so natural, so real, the two of them, side-by-side, on the way to his pickup after a nice dinner out.

For a moment, she wondered if they were getting in too deep. But then she knew she was just being silly. They were helping each other to reach their goals, plain and simple—and they might as well have a great time while they were at it.

They rounded the corner and strolled along the sidewalk, turning into the driveway that led to the parking lot. When they reached his pickup, he pulled open her door for her, waiting until she'd boosted herself into the seat and then closing it for her.

When he climbed in behind the wheel, he turned to meet her eyes and asked, "What now?"

There was a moment. They looked at each other and neither looked away—and why should they look away? It felt good to be sitting here in the parking lot behind Castillo's, lost in Graham Callahan's velvet-brown eyes.

"You were terrific tonight." His voice was low, rough in the most seductive way. It stroked along her nerve endings, making her whole body feel supersensitized.

She drew a slow, careful breath. "Yeah. It went really well and I had a great time."

"Me, too."

"I think you've got the votes of the entire Castillo family."

"We'll see. The election's not till November. Way too much can happen between now and then." He was staring out the windshield, his expression almost sad. Then he turned to her again—and frowned.

"What's wrong?" she asked.

"Not a thing. Why?"

"I don't know. As a rule, you're the most happy, self-confident guy I've ever met. But just now, you looked so thoughtful, so serious…"

Damn, Graham was thinking as he had a thousand times already tonight. *This girl is something special.*

Gorgeous, fun, smart—and way too perceptive. Every moment he spent with Cassie Trent was better than the last. So good, in fact, that he was already wanting to kick things up a notch, imagining how great it could be to make the best of the days they might have together—and wondering if she could possibly be thinking along those same lines.

He felt like he knew her so well—though really, it had only been a week since they'd met up by chance at the Silver Spur Café. The embarrassing truth was, she was ten steps ahead of him most of the time. And he loved it.

Plus, it didn't hurt at all that she was so nice to look at—scratch that. It did hurt. He was aching to do more than what their fake relationship allowed. It wasn't enough now to hold her hand and put his arm around her in public. He wanted to get up close and dangerously personal when there was no one else around. Not touching her for real and in private only got harder with every second he spent with her.

"Graham?" she asked, a grin pulling at the corner of that wide, soft mouth of hers.

"Uh. Yeah?"

"You're staring."

He nodded slowly. "Yes, I am—and we should get going…"

That grin of hers turned downright devilish. She knew exactly what he had on his mind. "It would probably be a bad idea," she said, continuing a conversation he didn't remember starting. "I mean, you and me getting too close in private, that would be…"

"A bad idea," he echoed. "Right…"

She caught her plump lower lip between her pretty white teeth and worried it gently. "It's not part of the plan, not what we agreed on."

"Plans change." He growled the words—though he hadn't meant to.

"We are fake, Graham. That was the plan. Displays of affection should be agreed on in advance and only executed in public."

"Right," he said, though it killed him to admit it. "You're right. I'm out of line to even be thinking about it. Forget that I…"

She cut him off by pressing two fingers against his lips. Her touch was heaven. Warm, tender, painfully sweet. He wanted to suck those two fingers right into his mouth. He *needed* to kiss her, and when he looked in her eyes he knew that she felt the same.

"You're *not* out of line." Her voice had gone husky.

"No?" He sure felt that way.

"Or if you are, well, I am, too." She pulled her hand away. It took all the will he possessed not to grab it back and press those fingertips to his mouth again. "Graham?"

"Yeah?"

"I think you'd better take me home."

"You got it." The words came out sounding curt,

though he hadn't intended them to. For a moment, he considered saying more.

But he kept his big mouth shut. They had an agreement, one that did not include intimate touching in private. There would be no deep, soulful, endless kisses—at least not when they were alone.

He started the truck and backed from the parking space.

All the way home to Stargazer Ranch, Cassie tried to come up with the right thing to say to him.

In the end, though, anything that came out of her mouth would have been wrong. She didn't want a real relationship, and adding benefits to their original agreement seemed dangerous in the extreme.

She turned her head toward the passenger window, shut her eyes and ordered herself not to think about having more with him. They were friends and there was chemistry—and chemistry was good for the plan. People believed they were a couple because they really liked each other, because the attraction between them was as real as it gets.

And sometimes, when they were together playing at their fake relationship for all they were worth, she couldn't help thinking that it didn't feel fake in the least.

Well, so what?

She needed *not* to go making a big deal out of this—and not to get down in the weeds with him about it, either. Talking the problem to death would solve nothing.

When he pulled up in front of the house and stopped the truck, she made herself give him a bright smile. "So here's what I think…"

He tossed his hat onto the back seat, turned his body

toward her and said bleakly, "You're backing out, aren't you?"

The question took her completely by surprise. "What? No!"

"You're not?" The hope in his voice made her want to grab him and hug him—but she didn't. She kept her greedy hands to herself.

"Of course not. I'm still in. I was just going to say that we need to stick with the original plan."

"No touching except in public, you mean?"

"Exactly."

He laughed, a humorless sound. "I'm going to look on the bright side."

"Which is?"

"I am so damned relieved you're not calling the whole thing off."

"I mean it, Graham. We really do need to keep our hands off each other when it's just you and me." She was reminding herself more than him.

"I get it." He blew out his cheeks with a heavy breath. "And I know you're right. I just don't like it."

"But can you live with it?"

"Guess I'll have to."

"Okay, then. We're good—now, about what's coming up…" She whipped out her phone. He just sat there, looking at her in a way that made her want to toss the phone over her shoulder and vault across the console into his lap. "Stop that," she warned.

That made him smile—a real smile. "Yes, ma'am." He pulled out his own phone. "Okay, Madame Campaign Manager, tell me where I have to be and when. I'll add it to my calendar."

"Hmm. It's not like we have a long list of events planned."

He was grinning. "Then just tell me what's next."

"Think about your platform. You've been handing out a flyer and it's great as far as it goes. But I think we need a brochure, don't you?"

He put on a wounded expression—but she knew him well enough by then to see that he was actually teasing her. "I thought my flyer was pretty good."

"It is. Didn't I just say that?"

"Yeah. But tell me again."

"Graham. It's the best flyer ever in the history of flyers—and we need a brochure."

"All right. I'll get on that. What else?"

"Campaign strategies."

"Okay…"

"And you need to keep knocking on doors."

"I've canvased half the businesses on Central Avenue."

"Excellent. Make a list of every business in town and visit the rest of them. It's not a big town. You can do it. I'll help."

"Damn. I am really taking advantage of you."

She faked a heavy sigh. "I like to think of it as my civic duty. Plus, hello. What's a campaign manager for?"

"Good point. Now I don't feel quite so guilty." He was looking at her—staring, really.

And she was staring right back at him. Suddenly, the big cab of his pickup was too small for the two of them. "I should go in."

His dark eyes held hers. "I was afraid you were going to say that. Are you free tomorrow?"

She should probably put a little space between them for a few days, at least. But he was looking at her so hopefully. Not to mention the fact that hanging out with him was a whole lot more fun than anything else she might end up doing.

Cautiously, she asked, "What exactly did you have in mind?"

"Campaigning, of course. You did say you'd help."

"Yes, I did." She tried not to notice the little zing of excitement in her chest at the idea that she was obligated to follow through on her promise to support his campaign. "Tomorrow, my morning's booked," she warned. "It's a ranch, after all. That means cattle, horses, chickens and goats—and *that* means I'm busy from dawn till early afternoon."

"Believe it or not," he said drily, "I am familiar with ranch life. So how about this? I'll spend a little time tonight working on my new brochure. I'll print copies and bring them with me when I pick you up at two. We'll make the rounds together, talk to the shop owners I haven't visited with yet about what I plan to do for this town."

"That could work." She was nodding. "We could go to a few stores together and then, once I have a feel for what to say, we could split up and spend a couple more hours covering twice as much ground. Depending on how long that takes, we can move on to knocking on doors, talking to people at home in whatever areas of town you haven't covered yet."

"It's a good plan—and then, as a thank-you, I'm taking you to dinner."

Dinner? She would love that—but come on. She'd promised herself that she would draw the line with him. "Honestly, Graham. Dinner's not necessary."

"Oh, yeah, it is. I can't let you campaign for me all afternoon and then send you home on an empty stomach."

Say you have plans, the voice of wisdom whispered in her ear. *Tell him you have a lot to do and none of it can be put off...*

She did no such thing. "Where would we go?" Castillo's again, most likely, she thought. The Silver Spur didn't serve dinner, and neither the Grizzly nor the Tenacity Social Club offered much in the way of food.

"Don't worry," he said. "I'll figure it out."

She made a half-hearted stab at backing out. "But Graham, I would need to be home by eight to milk my goats."

"I'll make sure to get you there in time. Now, say yes. I'll take care of the rest—because we really do need to talk about our progress after we finish canvasing."

Oh, why not? she thought. She liked him and it was only dinner. "All right, then. Dinner sounds really nice."

When Graham pulled to a stop in front of the main house on Stargazer Ranch at two the next afternoon, Cassie and her mom were standing on the porch. Cassie, looking smoking-hot in tight jeans, a snug red shirt and red boots to match, had seen him drive up. She raised a hand to let him know she'd be down in a minute.

As though he would simply sit in the truck and wait for her to come to him. No way. Especially not with her mom standing right there.

He jumped out and headed up the steps. Cassie scowled as he approached. That just made him smile all the wider. "Afternoon, ladies." He swept off his hat.

"Hello, Graham!" Olive Trent greeted him with a whole lot of enthusiasm. "Cassie was just telling me of your plans for the day. Campaigning—and then dinner."

"That's right, Mrs.—"

"Olive," she corrected.

He nodded. "Olive it is. Cassie's helping me out and I really do appreciate it. I have to admit, I'm starting to depend on her. She has great ideas for the campaign."

Olive beamed at her daughter. "I'm so proud of you, honey."

Cassie looked like she was suppressing a sarcastic remark. "Thanks, Mom. And as I said, I'll be back by eight."

"Uh-uh." Olive wasn't going for it. "As *I* said just a few minutes ago, you don't have to worry about the goats. I will do the milking tonight. You and Graham will be working all afternoon for the good of this town. Once your work is done, you deserve a little time to relax and enjoy your dinner. There is no need to rush home."

"But—"

"Go on, now." Olive made a shooing motion with the back of her hand. "Do good work and have a nice time afterward."

"Okay, Mom," Cassie said far too patiently. Graham offered his arm. Cassie took it, but not before slanting him a look of pure suspicion.

"Thank you for taking care of the goats tonight, Olive," he said.

"It is my pleasure, Graham."

Cassie waited until they were driving away to grumble, "You better watch out. My mother wants me married. And right now, you are the prime candidate for the role of my groom. Scratch that. You're the *only* candidate. You need to be very, very afraid."

"So then." He grinned. "You owe me."

She gave him a look of sheer disbelief. "And you came to that conclusion, how?"

"Easy. As long as you and I are spending time together, your mom is off your back."

"My mother is never truly off my back."

"Oh, yes she is. She's happy when she sees you and me together, and she's going to be happy for months because we're going to be seeing a lot of each other until the election in November. Plus, what about that deal you made with her for bringing a date to Renee's wedding? Isn't that deal supposed to last for a full year?"

"Yes, it is. But she likes you. A lot. And that makes me nervous. Who knows what she'll do after the election when you're no longer in the picture…"

"What's that old saying? Let's cross that bridge when we come to it. The election is months away. Live in the moment and let the future take care of itself."

"Oh, this is not going to end well," she muttered darkly.

"Cassie…"

She huffed out a hard breath. "What?"

"Think of it this way."

"Which way is that?"

"We are going to have a whole lot of fun while it lasts."

"Where are you taking me?" Cassie asked at a little after six that evening.

For the past several hours, at first together and later separately, they'd visited businesses and homes all over town. Now he was supposed to be taking her to dinner—which, apparently, was going to happen somewhere on his family's ranch. She knew this because he'd just stopped to open the gate with the rustic Callahan Canyon Ranch sign above it.

"We're having a picnic," he said as he jumped back in a second time after closing the gate behind them.

"Don't you need food for that?"

"I have food. It's in the back seat."

She craned her head back there and saw a cooler behind the driver's seat and a picnic basket tucked behind her seat. "You came prepared."

"It was either that or Castillo's—which is always good, but we *were* there just last night." He shut the door, buckled himself back in, and they set off again. "Tonight, you have your choice of sitting on my front porch or on a blanket at my favorite spot by Callahan Creek."

"Hmm. It's a difficult decision. But I'll take the picnic by the creek."

"You got it."

"And I didn't know that you had your own house."

"I do. So does Colter. Archer and Ash share the main house."

Cassie knew that Graham's dad, Colter, Sr., had died when the brothers were boys. His mom, Arleta, had taken over the running of Callahan Canyon and finished raising her boys on her own. She'd died three or four years ago—in the winter, if Cassie remembered right. Nowadays, Arleta's grown sons ran the family spread together.

The graveled road branched into two dirt roads. He took the one that veered away from the buildings.

They bounced along. On the right, they passed the opening to the steep-walled canyon that gave the ranch its name. The big truck downshifted as they climbed a hill. At the gentle crest, she could see the creek below them. Mature-growth cottonwoods, tall and green, rose from the creek bank, leaves rustling in the early-evening breeze.

Graham drove up another slight rise and then down toward the twisting ribbon of gleaming water. He stopped a short distance from the stream. They got out. Cassie grabbed the wicker picnic basket. He took the cooler from behind the driver's seat and got a rolled-up blanket from the lockbox in the bed behind the cab.

It was a short walk to a nice, grassy spot several feet from the water. Graham spread the blanket. By then it was almost seven, still daylight, but the shadows were growing longer. There was beer in the cooler. For the meal, he'd brought chicken wraps and pasta salad.

"Yum!" she said. "Who put all this together?"

He looked pleased and said modestly, "I did."

"This is great. I am so impressed."

"Well, I'm on my own at my place, and I do like to eat."

She took a bite of the chicken wrap. The chicken was grilled to perfection and there was plenty of shredded cheese, lettuce and just the right amount of ranch dressing. She raised her beer to him. "Here's to the chef."

"Thank you—there are barbecue chips in the basket."

She set down her beer and her wrap to open the bag of chips. He took one and munched on it as she admired the wicker basket with its fold-back wicker lid and its red-and-white-checked lining. "This basket is a classic. I love it."

"It was my mom's. After she died, I stole it from the main house. My brothers still give me a hard time about that."

"Why?"

"Because that's what brothers do—but nobody's demanded I put it back. They just razz me for being sentimental." He looked sad.

She had to resist the urge to reach out and squeeze his shoulder—in reassurance, or maybe comfort. She wasn't sure which. "Your mom used this basket a lot, then?"

"Yeah. She was big on picnics. She always said that a picnic makes a day feel special. Once or twice a week in the warmer months, she would pack up that basket and pile us all into one of the ranch trucks.

"We had picnics at just about every decent spot along this creek—and in the canyon, too. My dad used to tease her for being so easy to please. He said she deserved caviar and fine wine. Instead, she got sandwiches and beer."

"The way I remember it, your mom was kind. And always smiling."

"Yeah. She made the best of any situation. And she was a tough one, too. My dad died when my brothers and I were pretty young…"

Cassie had heard how Colter, Sr. died. He'd been bucked off a horse, hit his head on a rock and died instantly. "I'm so sorry about your dad."

Graham gave her a rueful hint of a smile. "It was a long time ago…"

"But still, it must have been awful for you."

"Yeah, it was tough for all of us. But Mom put on a brave face and kept going. We all pitched in as best we could to keep the operation afloat—even Archer. He was seven at the time. Like the rest of us, Archer could ride by the age of five. When my dad died and it was just my mom and us boys, Archer would feed the chickens and gather the eggs. Whatever needed doing, he was willing…" Graham's voice trailed off. Then he seemed to shake himself. "Anyway, what I'm saying is, we got by. My mom had this way of making it all fun and exciting. I don't know how she did it. But no matter how tough things got, she always looked on the bright side of any situation."

Cassie sipped the last of her beer and stared at the creek that burbled along not far from the blanket where they sat. She'd heard that his mom had died of a sudden, severe case of pneumonia. It made her ache for him and his brothers, to have lost both their parents already. Cassie couldn't imagine her life without her dad in it.

And sometimes her mom made her want to climb the walls, but still… Olive Trent supported her children unconditionally. Cassie probably needed to be more appreciative of her mom's fierce and unwavering devotion.

"Hey," Graham said.

"Hmm?" She met his eyes.

"Somehow, I've taken the evening to a very dark place."

She blinked and turned to him. "No, you haven't. I was just thinking that life can be really tough sometimes, that's all."

Their gazes met and locked. He whispered, "Yes, it surely can."

Far off toward the mountains, she heard the cry of a hawk. Glancing up, she spotted the bird as it sailed on the thermal winds high above. The sky was changing, hints of the coming twilight layering the darkening blue with orange and purple and red.

When she shifted her gaze to Graham again, he was watching her. She teased, "Is it time to discuss the progress of the campaign?"

He gave a slow nod. "You are so right. We should do that now. The campaign is going great guns. Let's keep up the good work."

She stared at him, waiting for more. When he just grinned at her, she demanded, "That's it? That's all?"

"What else is there to say?"

She should probably argue with him, tell him not to be too sure of himself. But he was right. They'd worked hard all day. They deserved to relax and enjoy the moment.

"Cassie?"

"Hmm?"

He leaned a little closer. She knew she should back away, put some distance between them.

But she didn't. She was too busy thinking how handsome he was, with those wicked dark eyes and that flirty smile. Somehow, he always managed to look like he was up to no good in the best sort of way.

And honestly, how could she back away when all she wanted to do was get closer?

"Cassie…" This time, he said her name on a low husk of breath.

"Graham…"

His lips met hers. She sighed and reminded herself that she needed to push him away.

But she didn't. Instead, she reached for him. He moved closer, wrapping her up in those lean, hard arms of his. Pulling her into the heat of his body, he lowered her gently to the blanket.

She thought, *This is a bad, bad idea.* But his kiss was *so* good. He made a low, desperate sound against her parted lips.

Cassie closed her eyes and forgot to think at all.

Chapter Six

Graham knew exactly what to do.

He needed to stop this. Now. They were friends and he liked her so much and this kiss he was stealing could end up ruining everything.

But his body seemed unwilling to listen to his brain. He cradled her close. Her sweet, fresh scent surrounded him. He kissed her slow and deep, and he wanted to go right on kissing her forever.

She was so slim and strong and womanly. He liked everything about her from her quick wit to her goats to her failed outdoor-movie side hustle. He admired her, loved the way she helped him out with his campaign, urging him to improve on his original flyer, canvasing all afternoon with him to get the word out.

She was something special, all right. And she said she didn't want a relationship any more than he did.

Did she really mean that?

Even if she did mean it, he ought to know better by now than to fool around with another local girl—especially one with a matchmaking mama, who was not going to be happy with him when he and Cassie parted ways.

However…

Damn.

She felt just right in his arms.

And realistically, Olive was bound to be disappointed in the end anyway. He and Cassie already knew where they stood with each other.

About then, she caught his face between her hands. He blinked and looked down at her. Those blue eyes, delectably glassy now, stared up at him.

Somehow, he managed to lift his mouth an inch from those sweet, tempting lips. He wanted to claim another kiss, to keep on kissing her, to never stop. He longed to lie here in the slowly gathering darkness, holding this woman in his arms for the rest of the night and on into Sunday morning as the creek burbled along a few feet away...

"Graham," she whispered up at him.

"Bad idea?" he asked. The question sounded rough and raw to his own ears.

Her sleek eyebrows drew together. "Yeah." She looked pained—but then she gave him a hint of a smile. "I mean, we did agree to keep things strictly hands off except for show..."

"You're right." He made himself pull away. Rising to his knees, he held out a hand. She took it and he pulled her to a sitting position. "I was out of line." He sank back on his heels.

She laughed then, a low, teasing sound that made his heart pound harder. "Okay, fine. You can have all the blame."

He groaned. "You're going to kill me, you know that?"

"Nah. And no matter how hard you try to make yourself the bad guy, you aren't the only one at fault for what just happened." She forked her fingers back through her shining hair. "I wanted to kiss you, Graham—and I did."

His heart stopped and then commenced beating double time. "Hey. I'm trying to do the right thing here, and you're not making it easy."

"Poor Graham." She clucked her tongue. "Trying so hard to be good."

"Don't be mean." He was pouting and he knew it.

But sweet heaven, she looked beautiful. Her mouth was swollen from his kiss, her hair a little wild, her eyes full of mischief and heat. She seemed to be daring him to reach out and wrap her up in his hungry arms all over again.

"Sorry," she said.

"No, you're not."

She granted him a shrug. "It's not just going to go away, you know."

"It?"

Now she looked at him patiently. "You know exactly what I mean. This." She pointed at him and then at herself. "This attraction between us. We need to be realistic. After all, the plan is that we'll be seeing a lot of each other until after the election."

"Right…" He drew the word out, not knowing where she was going with this—and doubtful he would like it when she got to the point.

"Instead of resisting this thing until we both give in, I think we need to talk about it frankly and honestly and then make a well-reasoned decision about what to do."

"Cassie."

"What?"

"Talking about it is only going to make it more likely to happen."

"And you don't want it to happen?" she asked, her head tipped to the side, a look he couldn't read in those unforgettable eyes.

"Are you kidding?" He groaned. "I want it to happen so bad it hurts."

"Me, too." She bit her lip. It was the sexiest thing he'd ever seen. His heart was going a mile a minute. He longed to reach out and grab her close—and honestly, shouldn't he have more self-control than this? They were a great team and the rapidly escalating attraction between them threatened to derail all their plans.

"So then," she went on. "I'm just going to put it out there. I propose that we add benefits to our fake relationship."

Her words stunned him. It took him a minute to respond. "You're serious…"

"Yes. A fling. A fling that will last until the election in November—or until one of us decides to opt out."

He stared at her for several seconds, his mind a dead blank. Then, finally, he declared in a carefully controlled tone, "You don't mean that."

"Yes, I do. It's ridiculous to keep saying we won't, to make agreements not to touch each other—and then grabbing each other and kissing each other like we'll never stop."

He was holding on to his limited store of scruples by a very slender thread. "Cassie. Think about it. Benefits are only going to make things more complicated."

"Oh, right, because they're not the least complicated already… Sheesh. Just be honest. Tell me it's a no."

He studied her face and thought that he'd never met anyone quite like her. So sunny and natural—and tough. And bold, too. She put it right out there and he liked that. A lot. "I just… Why the change of heart?"

"Because I would like it better if we could be honest with each other. Saying we're keeping hands off just isn't working. I'm not planning a future with you, I promise you. It would be a fling, and it would be over in November—and don't look at me like that.

"I promise I will not suddenly decide that you're my true, forever love. When the time comes, I will walk away just like you will. I know this because I've been with three men in my life, and each one of those men was supposed to be *the one*. They weren't. I've learned my lesson. I know who I am."

Three men. Who were they? He only recalled the one, the last one, the famous saddlemaker, Jake McGeorge...

She was shaking her head. "I am single and I'm staying that way." She frowned. "What are you thinking? Talk to me. If the answer is no, just say so. My pride might be wounded, but believe me, I'll survive. And we can move on."

He did think it was a bad idea. A hot, delicious bad idea. And he had an obligation to lay all his cards right out on the table. "Just to be up-front and honest, I'm not changing my mind on the relationship thing."

"Graham," she said patiently. "The horse is dead. Stop beating it. I believe you. I just want something sweet and fun and good. And only for a little while."

"Damn, Cassie."

She gulped. "What?"

"I'm in."

They stared at each other. He kept his mouth shut. It seemed wiser to let her set the pace.

She folded her hands in her lap, looked down at them and then back up at him. "You should take me home now."

His heart stopped—and then lurched to life again, beating fast and hard. Had he blown it somehow? It sure looked that way. Disappointment settled in his belly, heavy as a block of lead. "I understand," he said, and tried really hard to mean it.

"I need…a little time, I guess." She was chewing her lip again.

He wanted her at lot. But at that moment he realized that he wanted her friendship even more. For the first time, he thought of how it might be after the election. They could end their fake romantic relationship as planned but still manage to remain friends.

It could happen. Maybe—although Olive Trent might just come after him with a shotgun when she learned they'd called it quits. But then, together, they would settle Olive down. After that, they could go on as before, just without the fake romance or the hot, sexy times.

He would miss the sexy times, but still. He could definitely picture himself as Cassie's lifelong friend.

She was frowning at him. "You should see your face. What *are* you thinking about?"

He shook himself. Because…what the hell? He was planning their future as forever friends—and they hadn't even enjoyed the sexy times yet.

Plus, right now, he needed to be understanding about her doubts. "Look," he said. "If you're having second thoughts—"

"No. I'm not. Honestly." Her eyes were steady, holding his. "But I think we should…sit with the idea for a bit. Make sure we're both completely on board."

It wasn't what he'd hoped to hear. Because now that he'd let himself say yes to the idea of being her lover, he didn't want to wait another minute to have her in his arms again.

But a little time to think it over wouldn't kill him. It only felt like it might.

"All right, then," he said. "I'll take you home."

* * *

"You *what*?" Vicky demanded.

It was four in the afternoon on Monday. Cassie sat across from her friend at the small kitchen table in Vicky's studio apartment above Tenacity Grocery. The studio was tiny, charming, a little run-down—and nothing like the big house on Juniper Road where Vicky had grown up.

Cassie picked up the glass of sparkling water Vicky had served her—but then set it down without taking a sip. "Look. I meant what I said when we talked last week. I like Graham. I really do."

"But you said you don't *like* like him."

"I don't. I mean, it's not ever going to go anywhere between us. Neither of us has any interest in a long-term commitment."

"And yet, that you like him is a valid reason to jump into bed with him?"

"Well, um…"

"*Um*, what?" Vicky made a get-to-the-point gesture.

"It's just that, besides liking each other, Graham and I have this mind-numbing chemistry, you know?"

Vicky blinked three times in rapid succession. "Mind-numbing chemistry? There's not supposed to be any of that. Cassie, it's fake. You said it was fake."

"It *is* fake. But, well, you know how these things go…"

"What I know is that fake is fake—so no, I *don't* know."

"Well, what I'm trying to say is that yes, it's fake. But Vicky, the sparks…" She made a show of fanning herself, hoping Vicky would finally get the message. But her friend only looked at her, waiting for more. "How else can I put this? The attraction between Graham and me is very, very real, and we're both done resisting it."

Vicky flopped back in her chair and groaned up at the

ancient shiplap ceiling. "Done? The only thing you're supposed to be done with is men."

"And I am done with men."

"And yet you're considering having a fling with your fake boyfriend."

"Because I really, really like him. I do. And Vicky, it's been three years since I've had sex with a guy. Sometimes lately I wonder if I'll ever have sex with another person again."

"When you give up men, you give up having sex with them. That's kind of the point."

Her best friend was right and Cassie knew it. She should tell Graham that an affair would be unwise in the extreme, that she'd been wrong to even suggest such a thing and they needed *not* to go there. But what she *should* do and what would most likely happen were two very different things. Because some temptations were just too powerful to resist. And Graham Callahan was one of those. "Can we change the subject?"

Vicky's dark eyes softened. "Of course—and you probably shouldn't be asking for romantic advice from me, anyway. In my book, all men are trouble. Including your fake boyfriend, Graham."

"Gotcha." She drank a sip of sparkling water. "Let's move on then?"

"Yes. Let's."

There was a silence. Cassie cast about for a noncontroversial subject—like Renee's upcoming wedding. She said, "The good news is we're all set for Saturday."

"Excellent," said Vicky. "I, for one, can't wait."

As her sister's maid of honor, Cassie had put together an overnight bachelorette getaway for Renee and her bridesmaids. The group was all family and included their brother Noah's fiancée, Lucy Bernard, and also Miles's sister, Rylee, who was driving in from Bronco for the shindig. Chrissy Parker, who was married to Miles's brother Hayes, was on board, too. And Vicky, of course. Cassie's lifelong best friend had always been family to the Trents.

The fun would happen at Calder Creek Ranch, a guest ranch with a rustic spa less than a two-hour drive from Tenacity. Dogs were welcome at Calder Creek Ranch—which meant that Renee could bring her constant companion, Buddy.

"We will pick you up at 8:00 a.m. Be ready."

"You know I will."

On Tuesday, Cassie spent most of her day clearing a badly clogged ditch on the northern boundary of Stargazer Ranch.

It was getting close to three that afternoon when she returned to the barn and sheds to put her tools away and hose down the ranch truck. Once that messy job was done, she put the old truck in the vehicle shed and set out for the main house on foot. She was halfway there when she spotted Graham's big pickup headed her way. He pulled to a stop beside her and leaned out the window. Tipping his hat, he granted her his best killer grin.

"I was just in the neighborhood," he said. His eyes said a lot more. He looked at her with real appreciation. She had no idea why. It had been a long day and ditch clearing was messy work. She looked like she'd been dragged through the mud—because she pretty much had. Still, he stared at her like she was the sexiest woman he'd ever seen.

Was he thinking about where they'd left things on Saturday? She certainly was. And those thoughts had her stomach going absurdly swooshy and her cheeks feeling suddenly much too warm.

"What's up?" she asked, trying her best to play it cool.

Before he could answer, Adelaide, one of her dwarf Nubian kids born that spring, popped up from his passenger seat. The little goat clambered over the console and into Graham's lap. Sticking her head out the window, she bleated, "Maa…"

Cassie didn't know what to think. "Are you kidnapping Adelaide?"

"Adelaide," he repeated. "I like it." He gave the kid a pat on the head and fondly trailed his fingers down one of her floppy ears. Adelaide tipped her nose up. Bleating some more, she nibbled at the palm of his hand. "And no, this isn't a kidnapping. I found her standing in the middle of the road just inside the gate." He was still looking right at Cassie, wearing that bad boy grin that had her thinking—again—of all the intimate activities they'd yet to share. "You've got mud on your nose," he remarked.

"Yeah, and that's not the only place, believe me." She aimed a scowl at the little goat. "How did you get out this time?" Adelaide responded with a smug couple of bleats and went back to fondly nibbling on Graham.

He tipped his head toward the passenger door. "Get in. I'll drive you to the goat pen."

"I'll get mud in your truck."

"So what? It never stays clean for long anyway." Holding Adelaide with one arm, he reached across the console with the other and pushed open the passenger door.

"You asked for it." She went around the front of the truck and got in. "Here. Give her to me."

He passed her the goat. Adelaide protested, but not

too much. Graham put the truck in gear. They circled the meadow and stopped by the back gate to the goat pen.

"So here's the deal," she said when he pulled the truck to a stop. "I can't really talk now. Goats are world-famous escapers. I need to deal with this problem immediately." It was true. But still, she felt a tug of regret to be sending him on his way when he'd only just got here. She cuddled the naughty Adelaide in her arms. "I've got to figure out how this little girl escaped and if any others got out, because then I'll need to track them down. And *then* I'll have to fix whatever hole she got out through."

"I'll help."

"Graham. You don't have to—"

"I know I don't." Those chocolate-brown eyes took her in—her dirty face and grimy work clothes, her tattered straw hat and her hair that had been pulled back in a low ponytail when she started out that morning but by now had mostly gotten loose and straggled on her shoulders.

She said, "It doesn't seem right to keep taking advantage of you."

"Sure it does. Come on, let me help."

How could she say no to that smile, those eyes? "Suit yourself."

"Believe me, I am."

"Maa..." agreed Adelaide. She always had to put her two cents in.

Forty-five minutes later, Adelaide was back in the pen from which—hallelujah!—no other goats had escaped. Plus, Cassie and Graham had replaced the woven wire on the section of fence Adelaide had squeezed through.

"Thanks for the help," Cassie said. She swept off her mud-spattered hat and raked her fingers through her tangled hair. "And now, I really need to go clean up."

He studied her face. "Let me take you to dinner to-night."

Yes! she thought, but somehow managed not to say. Vicky's warnings from yesterday scrolled through her head. "Graham, I—"

"Hey. One way or another, you have to eat. Castillo's? I'll pick you up at six."

She did not want to get into their private business at Castillo's. Half the town would be there. "How about if I come to you?"

He looked surprised. But in a pleased kind of way. "My house, you mean?"

"What? Bad idea?" It probably was. But at least they would be able to talk in private.

"No. Not bad at all. Six? I can throw some steaks on the grill."

"I would like that. I'll bring wine and dessert—don't argue. I want to bring something."

"That sounds good. Hop in. I'll drive you back around to the house."

"Thanks, but my mom is home."

They stood close together just outside the goat pen. His dark eyes held hers and she could hear the echo of her heartbeat in her ears.

"Great. I like your mom."

"And she *loves* you."

One corner of that sexy mouth kicked up. "That's good."

"I suppose. But if you take me to the house, she's going to want to talk your ear off. You'll never get away, and I'll either have to stand there covered in mud, smiling through gritted teeth while she chatters on, or she'll dismiss me so I can clean up and then keep you there until I come back. Then she'll start in on you about staying for dinner. We don't want that, now, do we?"

He frowned. "We don't?"

"No, we do not. We're having dinner at your house, just the two of us..." Was her voice sounding strangely seductive?

Well, it had been a long day, and she did not want to stand around covered in mud while her mother gushed all over Graham.

Now he was grinning. "You're right. Just the two of us. Steaks and wine."

"Exactly."

"So," he said, "to get to my house, once you're through the main gate, just stay on the same road. It'll take you to a circle of three houses. Mine's the last one, a two-story log cabin. See you at six?"

"I'll be there," she promised, and realized that, however things went that night, she was looking forward to getting a little one-on-one time with him.

Graham and Izzy were waiting on the front steps when Cassie pulled up at his place that evening.

He would have gone to meet her, but Cassie jumped out fast and came right to him. "Who's this?" she asked when the border collie got up on all four paws and looked at their visitor with a wagging tail and an eager whimper of greeting.

"This is Izzy."

"Hey." Cassie crouched to scratch the dog around her furry black-and-white ruff. "You are gorgeous," she said. Izzy moaned in sheer happiness at the compliment—or maybe the attention.

Graham enjoyed the moment. Cassie looked great as

always, in snug faded jeans with a concho belt and a crop top that showed off a strip of her smooth, toned belly. He could hardly believe she was here, with him, at his place for the evening.

No matter what happened next, it was all good.

She rose to her feet again and looked up at the two-story cabin built of red cedar logs. "Did you build this house yourself?"

He stuck his hands in his pockets and tried to look modest. "I helped." She nodded, reaching down to give the quivering Izzy another quick pat on the head. He explained, "I had a little money when I moved back from Seattle five years ago. I put some of it away and invested some, too. But I really wanted my own place, and I always dreamed of living in a log cabin, so I hired a family friend from up near Rust Creek Falls to build this house." In northwestern Montana, Rust Creek Falls was fifty miles or so from the Canadian border. "My friend's got a small company that specializes in log homes—and come on in. I'll give you the tour. It won't take long."

"Hold on." Turning for the passenger door of her pickup, she pulled it wide to take out a bottle of red and a Tupperware container. "Wine and dessert, as promised." She handed the goodies to him.

He sniffed at the container. "Do I smell chocolate?"

"Yes, you do. Mom started baking as soon as I told her I was going to your place for dinner. Espresso chocolate chip cookies."

"Olive is the best."

"That she is," Cassie said with a sigh.

They went up the steps to the porch and he ushered her inside to his small front hall. "The primary bedroom is here on the main floor to the left," he explained.

"This way…" He went right and she followed him into the galley-type kitchen. A counter marked it off from the living area. He gestured broadly beyond the counter. "As you can see, there's the great room, the stairs to the second floor and over there on the far wall, the doors to the back deck."

"It's beautiful, Graham."

He felt a swell of pride at her praise. "Thanks. It's not real big, but there are two small bedrooms upstairs along with the main one down here. I have room for visitors— and nieces and nephews, too, if I ever get any of those."

She eyed the natural stone fireplace and the rustic stairs that led to the upper floor. "Your friend the log home builder is an artist."

"He knows his stuff, all right." Graham set the cookies on the counter and she handed him the wine. He got out a corkscrew, opened the bottle and poured them each a glass. They went out onto the back deck, where he had the grill going.

Half an hour later, they sat down at the picnic table under a big bur oak not far from the deck.

"So good," she said at her first bite of filet. "Here's to the grill-meister." She tapped her glass to his.

As dark came on, they moved to the deck swing to munch her mom's terrific cookies and finish the last of the wine. "These cookies are perfect with Cabernet," he declared.

"So true…"

"And I've got more wine inside," he said. "What do you say to another bottle?"

She shook her head slowly. "This is just right. Another bottle would be overkill. After all, at some point I'm going to need to get myself home." He tried not to hope too hard that she might stay over. "My mom is milking the goats again." She gave him a look of equal parts irony and humor. "As long as I'm out with you, she's happy to do it."

"Did I mention I love your mom?"

"I believe you might have, and more than once." With a tiny sigh, she lowered her head to his shoulder. "We have our differences, Mom and me. But overall, you're right. She's pretty great."

He dared to wrap his arm around her. Through the rustling leaves of the oak a few yards away, he could see the half-moon hanging there in the star-thick Montana sky. At their feet, Izzy wagged her tail against the deck boards.

When Cassie tipped her beautiful face up to him, he lowered his mouth and she lifted hers a fraction higher. Their lips met. She opened for him so sweetly. Their kiss tasted of chocolate and the richness of the wine.

He was in heaven. Whatever happened next, he felt like the luckiest man alive, just to have her here with him right now.

She pressed her hand against his chest. Reluctantly, he lifted his mouth from hers.

Her eyes were midnight blue. "Graham…"

"Talk to me," he said.

She touched the side of his face and whispered, "About those benefits we discussed…"

He tried really hard not to get his hopes up. "Yeah?"

"I want them."

His heart did a forward roll inside his chest. But somehow he kept himself in check and met her gaze steadily. "Are you sure?"

She wrapped her slim fingers around the back of his neck and pulled him closer, until their lips almost touched. "Yes." She breathed the word against his mouth.

And then she kissed him.

Chapter Seven

Graham took Cassie's hand and led her inside. Izzy was close on their heels.

"Stay," he said gently. With a small whine of disappointment, Izzy dropped to her haunches in front of the fireplace.

Graham pulled Cassie across the wide-plank cedar floor and into the hallway that led to his bedroom. The moment they were over the threshold, he gathered her into his arms again. As he kissed her, he kicked the door shut behind them.

A soft moan escaped her when he caught her lower lip lightly between his teeth and bit down just a little. They were both breathing hard.

But then she clasped his shoulders and broke the kiss. Her eyes were so big, the pupils blown wide. "I'm, uh, not on birth control…"

He captured her left hand and brought it to his lips. "I have condoms. Is that okay for you?"

Staring up at him, she gulped. The look on her face was priceless. Scared. Determined. Brave. Wild. "Yeah, that'll do," she said on a husk of breath.

"So we're still on?"

"Graham Callahan, we are most definitely on."

He pulled her close. Surging up, she pressed her lips to his.

He smiled against her mouth and wished he could go on kissing her forever as she wrapped herself around him and lifted closer with a little jump. He took the hint. Sliding his hands under her thighs, he boosted her up so she could hook her boots at the small of his back.

Kissing her deeply, thrilled at the feel of her body pressed good and tight to his at last, he carried her to his bed and then just stood there, lost—in her kiss, in the feel of her long fingers stroking the nape of his neck, in the scent of her, so clean and sweet.

He loved it, kissing Cassie. He could stand here holding her, kissing her, breathing her in for eternity—and longer. The rest of the world could spin on by without them. Right now, it felt entirely possible that he could spend forever in this room, holding Cassie Trent tightly in his arms.

She was the one who pulled back. When he opened his eyes she was watching him. She grinned at him.

He laughed and so did she. She squirmed a little. Reluctantly, he let her feet slide to the floor.

She plunked down on the bed and then fell back across it, spreading her arms wide. He knelt, eased between her knees and took off her boots for her. She wore red socks, which pleased him no end—why, he had no clue. He pulled them off, one and then the other, and threw them over his shoulder, heedless of where they might land.

Rising, he jumped on one foot and then the other, getting out of his own boots and socks. She started to take off her shirt.

"Wait," he said. "Let me help."

"Go for it." She grinned and spread her arms wide again.

So he climbed onto the bed and up over her. On his knees above her, he stared down into her eyes.

She gazed up at him dreamily as he slid off her concho belt and tossed it behind him. It landed on the rug with a cheerful clatter. Next, he undid the button at the top of her jeans. Then he took the zipper down, backing off the bed in the process.

She lifted those slim hips to help him as he pulled off her jeans and tossed them away. Her panties went with them. They were the hipster kind—red, sprinkled with tiny white stars.

She was pure temptation, lying there with her yellow hair fanned out across the patchwork quilt, wearing her cropped shirt with nothing below it.

The little triangle of short, silky dark gold hair at the apex of her thighs beckoned him. He bent close and pressed a quick, nipping kiss there. She gave him a gasp followed by a soft little sigh. And then she sat up and scooted back to rest against the pillows at the head of the bed. He caught her right ankle in his left hand.

She laughed, soft and sweet. And then, well, it seemed only right to kiss his way up the inside of her calf, to press his lips to the silky bend of her knee, to scatter more kisses along the smooth length of her inner thigh.

"Graham…" She whispered his name on a low moan. "Yes, just like that…"

"Oh, yeah, just like this," he agreed, rough and low, moving back from her a little, taking hold of both ankles and pulling her down so she was flat on her back again.

Sliding his hands under those pretty thighs, he guided them over his shoulders. She opened for him and he took shameless advantage, kissing her endlessly, using his tongue and his fingers and even, very gently, his teeth.

When she cried out and balled the quilt in her fists, he stuck with her. She pulsed so sweetly against his tongue, crying his name like it was the only name she'd ever known.

Finally, she went limp with a soft, sweet sigh. He nuzzled those gold curls one last time and then lifted his head.

"Graham..." She whispered his name so softly now, reaching down to gently comb his hair back off his forehead with her fingertips. "Graham," she said again with a happy little sigh.

He scooted up her body and wrapped her in his arms. It was a magical moment, just the two of them, holding each other, face-to-face. Lying with her like this, he could so easily imagine how good it might be to spend every night right here in his bed with her.

But no.

That was never going to happen. They understood each other, and neither of them would be bringing up the possibility of forever.

With a soft, contented sound, she eased free of his arms and took off her crop top and her bra. Then, naked and so charmingly comfortable in her own skin, she reached for him once more.

As their lips met in a hungry kiss, she got to work unbuttoning his shirt, sliding it off his shoulders and dropping it over the side of the bed, then quickly pulling his undershirt up and off, as well. He shoved off his boxer briefs and sent them flying.

"Come on," she said. Pulling him with her, she went up to her knees. Kneeling there in the center of the tangled quilt, they kissed for the longest, sweetest time.

And then things got urgent.

She opened her eyes. He stared into them, mesmerized. In a hushed voice, she asked, "Condom?"

"Got it…" He let her go to open the bedside drawer and hold up what they needed. She took it from him and removed the wrapper. He groaned as she rolled it down over him.

And then she put her lips to his ear. "Lie down, Graham…"

He couldn't get prone fast enough.

A moment later, she was hitching a leg over him. He stared up at her flushed, sweet face and decided he just might be the luckiest man alive.

Bending close, she guided him to her. Their eyes held. At some point, he realized he'd forgotten to breathe so he sucked in a long gulp of air.

She braced her hands on his chest. Her eyes locked with his, she murmured his name low and sweet. He surged up into her.

After that, time spun away. He completely lost track of everything but the feel of her above him, the sight of her gorgeous, flushed face as she took him. They moved together, two waves in an ocean of endless sensation.

He watched her, loving the way she gave herself over to the moment. Could they make this pleasure last forever? He fervently wished that they might.

But then it happened. She threw her head back and cried out her completion. When she collapsed on top of him, he cradled her close, matching his breathing to hers, aware of everything about her—her breasts pressed against him, her blond hair trailing along his arm, tickling just a little, the way she reached for his hand, wove their fingers together and, for a long, sweet moment, held on tight.

Finally, with a happy sigh, she sat up—and started moving again, rocking against him, driving him higher.

He didn't last long after that. Yanking her down to him, wrapping his arms around her, holding on for dear life, he lifted his hips, surging up even deeper into her as he felt himself go flying over the edge. With a long, hard groan, he captured her mouth and kissed her wildly as his finish roared through him.

A gentle hand brushed Cassie's cheek.

"Hey, sleepyhead," Graham whispered.

She was drifting free, feeling limp and so relaxed, completely satisfied. He'd left the bed a little while ago. She'd slid under the covers and closed her eyes...

He touched her shoulder. She blinked up at him. He stood beside the bed without a stitch on. Bending close, he pressed his warm lips to her cheek. "Cassie..."

"Hmm?"

They shared a smile. She let out a soft sigh of pure appreciation. Graham Callahan was every cowgirl's sexiest dream—with or without his clothes.

His sweet border collie appeared beside him. Cassie rolled to her side and reached out. "Hey, pretty girl..." Izzy wagged her feathery tail as Cassie gave her a nice, long scratch around her ruff.

Graham ran his hand down the dog's back. "Okay, now. Go lie down." Izzy headed for the dog bed near the door to the hallway.

"Scoot over?" Graham asked.

Moving back from the edge of the bed, Cassie lifted the covers to make room for him. He slid between the sheets and pulled her into his arms. His body felt just right pressed to hers. She rested her head on his lean, broad chest.

"I should go," she said sleepily.

"Not yet. It's only a little past nine…"

She pushed up on an elbow to blink down at him. "Morning comes early at Stargazer Ranch."

"I hear you." Reaching up, he guided a hank of hair back behind her ear. His smile was full of mischief.

She looked down at him warily. "What?"

He faked a serious expression. "I think you broke me."

She laughed at that, letting her head droop toward him until their foreheads touched. "Buck up," she advised in her tough-girl voice. "You'll live." His mouth was right there. She kissed him.

Surprise, surprise. She never wanted to stop.

But then he caught her face between his hands. "Lie here with me," he said. "Just for a little while."

As if she could refuse such a sweet invitation. She cuddled in close with her head on his shoulder.

He asked in a lazy voice, "So, are you ready?"

She tipped her head back to give him a look of playful disdain. "Again? You're such an animal."

He pulled her a little bit closer and she didn't mind at all. "Believe it or not, at the moment I'm not talking about sex." He brushed a kiss at her temple.

"Oh?"

"Nope. Right now, I'm talking about the stuff we haven't told each other, about the *L*-word and why you want nothing to do with it."

"I'm not the only one," she reminded him.

He took her hand, turned it over and kissed the center of her palm. "Fair's fair. You want me to go first?"

She made a show of thinking it over. "You did say that you would, remember?"

He seemed to consider the idea. But then he balked. "I don't know. Maybe not tonight…"

That was just fine with her. But she razzed him anyway. "Hey, I'm not the one who brought it up."

"You're right. I want to know everything about you, and I'm willing to tell you my story in return—but then I'm not."

She smiled down at him, thinking again how handsome he was—while at the same time reminding herself that this was just for now, a trade-off. They were using each other for their own separate reasons, not laying the foundations for a life together.

Really, there was no need to go wallowing around in the disappointments of the past. She didn't have to know why he'd sworn off love. And no way he needed to hear about what had happened with Butch and Craig and Jake.

"Okay, then," she said. "Let's not talk about the past tonight. Let's discuss what just happened instead."

"It was good," he said roughly. "Very good."

"I completely agree." She touched his arm under the covers, trailing her fingers from the bulge of his triceps to the bones of his wrist.

"I think we should take full advantage of this thing we've got going on between us." His voice was low and sandpaper rough.

"Oh, yeah?"

"Yeah. I'm all for benefits with you, Cassie Trent…" He hesitated, suddenly bashful. She liked him even more for that, for the way he backed off and didn't push too hard. "I mean, if you feel the same?"

She pretended to have to think it over. "Hmm…"

He groaned. "You're killin' me here."

"Don't die on me, please." She leaned in and kissed him, a quick peck that turned into something longer and deeper. He was such a good kisser. She could lie here kissing him till morning, she really could.

Gently backing away to the other pillow, she said, "As for benefits, I agree. We should enjoy all the perks of this temporary relationship of ours."

"Just what I was hoping you might say..." He pulled her back into the warm circle of his arms.

With a happy little sigh, she snuggled in close, resting her head on his shoulder and letting her eyelids drift shut. *Just for a moment*, she thought...

Cassie's eyes popped open. "What time is it?" she demanded of the shadowed ceiling overhead.

Beside her, Graham stirred. "Dunno," he replied sleepily. "I'll check..." He shifted away and the light on the far side of the bed popped on.

Cassie didn't wait for him to feel around for his phone. She glanced toward the shut blinds and thought she saw the beginnings of daylight around the edges.

"Oh, no!" Scrambling from the bed, she freed her jeans from the pile of clothes on the rug and fished in the pocket. "I don't believe this," she groaned when the screen of her phone lit up. "It's six-fifteen."

"Can't be," Graham muttered. "I never sleep that late."

She turned to him as he pushed back the covers, swung his legs to the floor and stood. They stared at each other. He really looked good naked, even with his dark hair standing up every which way and a sleep crease on his beard-scruffy cheek.

Those dark eyes of his were checking her out in return. "Good morning," he said with a wicked grin.

"Morning." She was groggy, frantic and aroused all at once. "I would love to stay, but I need to go."

As she got to work separating the rest of her wrinkled clothes from his, he offered, "Coffee?"

"That would be great. Got a travel mug I can borrow?"

"Yes, I do. Throw me my pants and I'll get the coffee maker going."

She tossed his Wranglers toward the bed and he caught them one-handed. A moment later, he left the room with Izzy close on his heels.

Cassie threw on her clothes. The good news was that her jeans and knit shirt looked none the worse for wear even after spending the night in a wad on the floor.

After she'd pulled on her socks and boots, she ducked into the bathroom to splash water on her face and run a comb through her tangled hair. Then she checked her phone again.

Not a peep from her mom. Was it possible that Olive Trent hadn't noticed that her younger daughter never came home last night?

Hah! Not a chance.

She knew why her mom hadn't called. Olive adored Graham and trusted him to take good care of her daughter. Cassie wasn't sure how she felt about that.

In the kitchen area, Graham was filling a travel mug with delicious-smelling coffee. "Cream? Sweetener?" he asked.

"A little milk if you have it."

He turned, pulled open the fridge and took out a quart of milk, which he set on the counter next to her coffee. "Help yourself."

"You are lifesaver." She added the milk, handed back the carton, stole one delicious sip from the mug and then put the lid on it.

They faced each other. She met those dark eyes and thought of the night before and felt just a little bit weak in the knees.

He said, "I'll be over," and then added ruefully, "probably this afternoon." He leaned back against the counter by the sink and gripped the edge behind him with both hands. His eyes told her everything. He was remembering last night, too. "I don't think I can stay away…" His voice was like heavy velvet stroking her skin.

She tried to look serious and doubtful about the wisdom of this fling they were now indulging in. Epic fail. Her careful frown lasted half a second. Before she could stop herself, she was grinning.

And he was grinning right back. They each took a step, which had them meeting in the middle of the narrow kitchen.

"Damn," he said, framing her face in his warm hands. "I don't want to let you go…"

She said nothing, just lifted her mouth to his.

They kissed for the longest time. Finally, with real regret, she pulled back. "Gotta move. There are eggs to gather and goats to milk—not to mention, my mother to deal with."

He handed her the travel mug. "There are six cookies left. I'm keeping them."

"I wouldn't have it any other way."

At home, Cassie hoped to sneak quietly in the door, race up the stairs, throw on old jeans and a work shirt and sneak back outside before her mother noticed she'd been there and gone.

Didn't happen. She was halfway up the porch steps when her mom pulled open the front door.

"There you are," Olive Trent said cheerfully. Her smile was nothing short of triumphant. "How's Graham?"

"He's great, Mom."

Olive put her hand over her heart. "I knew this would happen."

"I have no idea what you're talking about," Cassie baldly lied.

"Oh, please, sweetheart. We're both adults here."

Yes, they were. And Cassie had zero desire to discuss last night with her mom. As she had more than once in the past few years, she reevaluated the wisdom of living in her mother's house.

"I need to change clothes and get to work." Cassie stated the obvious in the hopes that Olive would leave well enough alone.

And what do you know?

She did. "Of course." Olive swung the door wide and gestured Cassie inside. Even better, she remained by the door as Cassie started up the stairs. "Scrambled egg sandwich on toast?" she offered.

Cassie paused halfway up. "Thanks, Mom." She meant it. Really, living with her mom wasn't *all* bad. Plus, her mom was always kind and thoughtful. And she wasn't judgmental. Yes, she wanted Cassie to find true, forever love and get a ring on it. But, as this morning proved, at least she didn't expect her grown daughter to live like a nun in the meantime. "An egg sandwich would be wonderful. I really am starving."

"Oh, sweetheart," Olive simpered, "I'm sure you are…"

* * *

Graham pulled up in front of the Trent house late that afternoon to find Cassie sitting on the front porch in dusty jeans and her tattered straw hat.

He turned off the engine, got out of the truck and climbed the steps to sit beside her. "Rough day?" he asked.

"Nothing out of the ordinary."

"Want to get something to eat and visit the Social Club?"

"Not tonight." She took off her hat and hit it on her thigh. Dust flew off it.

"I know a good swimming hole on Callahan Creek."

She looked right at him then and smiled slow and sweet. "Now you're talkin'."

He felt like a million bucks, just to have made her smile after a long day of hard work. "Get your suit."

She leaned his way and nudged him with her shoulder. "My mom's inside."

"I'll just come on in to say hi to her."

"Oh, you are a charmer, Graham Callahan."

"I try—after the swim I'll fix us some dinner at my house."

"Plus, you cook. You better watch out. My mom will never let you get away."

"Should I be scared?"

"You should be terrified."

But he wasn't. Not in the least. He followed her inside and spent a few minutes with Olive while Cassie ran upstairs to change. As before, Cassie's mom seemed really glad to see him. He knew he should probably avoid the woman because she clearly had plans for him—plans that centered on Cassie wearing his ring. Would Olive hate him come November?

He hoped not. She seemed a reasonable woman who, in the end, would see that Cassie was bound to make her own choices in life. And that getting married wasn't going to be one of them—not to him, anyway.

Cassie came down the stairs in record time wearing clean jeans and a different shirt—over her swimsuit, he assumed. She had a canvas pack slung on one shoulder. "Back by eight, Mom. Promise. I'll milk the goats myself."

Olive waved a hand. "No worries. Stay later if you want to. I'll handle the milking."

Cassie said firmly, "Thanks, but I'll be home in time to do it myself."

Outside, Cassie insisted on following him in her own pickup, which probably meant that she really would be heading home before eight. He tried not to be too disappointed.

They stopped at his house so he could put on a pair of swim trunks and then she got in his crew cab with him for a quick, bumpy ride to his favorite swimming hole along Callahan Creek.

He spread a saddle blanket on the bank for them. Cassie shed her jeans and shirt to reveal a hot pink racerback swimsuit. He immediately wanted to peel it off her and hoped really hard that he might get to do that before she went home.

They swam for a while and then sat on the blanket to dry off a little. She stretched out on her back and closed her eyes. He rolled to his stomach and propped himself up on his elbows beside her.

"Any chance you can go door-to-door with me on Saturday to talk about the election with folks on the east side of town?"

Shading her eyes with her hand, she looked up at him

with a rueful smile. "Sorry, but I can't. Saturday we're throwing Renee's bachelorette party. It's a spa thing over near Bronco. Massages, facials, mani-pedis, lots of girl talk. We won't be back till Sunday."

He felt a completely unacceptable tug of resentment that he probably wouldn't see her this weekend—and tried his best to ignore it. "You'd rather get pampered than help me drum up votes?"

She dismissed his question with a shrug. "Hey, I'm the maid of honor. The bachelorette party is my responsibility and I take that very seriously."

"I suppose that means I'm going to be stuck canvassing alone."

"You should get one of your brothers to go with you."

"Unfortunately, I can't see that happening—ever. My brothers are not real big on politics."

"Just a thought. But anyway, my weekend is booked."

For a fake boyfriend, he was feeling pretty damn let down at that news. He wanted every moment he could get with her. "How about tomorrow evening we grab a quick burrito at Castillo's and then head on over to the Tenacity Social Club?"

She grinned up at him. He really wanted to kiss those soft, pink lips of hers. "Right," she said. "People need to see us together so they know our love is true."

"Er, exactly."

"Just one problem, though. My mom's going to be taking care of the goats on her own while I'm off with Renee and the other bridesmaids at Calder Creek Ranch—and that means I wouldn't feel right taking advantage of her tomorrow night, too. I need to be home on time to milk my goats."

So much for luring her to his bed after their evening

out. But at least they would have a few hours together. "Got it. I promise to get you home by eight."

"In that case, it's a date. Tomorrow, then. Castillo's *and* the Tenacity Social Club."

"Now, that's what I wanted to hear." He rolled to his back, felt for his hat on the corner of the blanket and propped it over the top half of his face to shade his eyes.

"It's nice here," she said.

"Peaceful," he agreed with a nod.

Her hand touched his on the blanket. He smiled to himself. And then she rolled toward him. He pushed his hat out of the way so he could see her. Her skin was still damp from their swim. She dropped a quick kiss on his lips.

"Let's go to your place," she whispered.

He reached up and guided a wet lock of hair behind her ear. "I thought you'd never ask."

They went to his house where he took her straight to his bed.

In no time, it was seven-thirty and she was getting up to go. With Izzy at his heels, he followed her down the front steps to her pickup. Missing her already, he caught her hand and pulled her close for a last kiss.

"I do have to go," she murmured against his lips.

"I know…" He released her.

And then he stepped back, pulled open the driver's door for her and shut it once she was settled in the seat. Hands in his pockets, he watched her drive away.

Minutes later, he was still standing there, staring off toward where her pickup had disappeared from his sight.

Chapter Eight

At a little before five the next afternoon, Cassie walked into Castillo's with Graham at her side. They enjoyed delicious burritos and chatted with Yolanda about the progress of the campaign. At six, they went on over to the Tenacity Social Club.

"Hey, you two!" Mike Cooper, behind the bar, signaled them over.

Graham pulled out a stool for her and then took the one beside it.

"Let me guess," said Mike. "One mojito and a whiskey rocks." Mike served their drinks and moved on down the bar to refill a couple of pitchers for customers at the tables. When he came back, he asked, "So how's the campaign going?"

"Excellent," said Graham. "I see you put my brochure on the board by the door...along with the ones for Ellis Corey, JenniLynn Garrett and the one and only Marty Moore."

"Yep," Mike said with a smile. "We've put up election information for all the mayoral candidates. We try not to play favorites. After all, the Social Club serves the whole community."

Graham joked, "Clearly we need a little more corruption around here."

Mike laughed, but then he grew serious. "Unfortunately, I think we've had plenty of that in Tenacity for way too long."

"Sad but true," muttered Cassie. She lifted her glass. "Here's to a brighter future for our town and everyone in it." Mike raised his club soda. Graham and several others at the bar held their glasses high, too.

And right then, a voice from one of the tables said, "Cassie! Hey!" It was Roslyn Ainsly. And surprise, surprise, she was sitting with four other women, including her bestie, Larinda Peach.

Both Larinda and Roslyn jumped up and came straight for the bar. Roslyn grabbed Cassie in a hug as Larinda exclaimed, "How great to see you here!" She turned to Graham. "And what do you know? Hello, Graham Callahan..."

"How're you doing, Larinda?" he asked somewhat warily.

"Oh, you know." Larinda waved a hand. "Same old, same old."

"Girl's night out?" Cassie asked.

"Yes!" replied Roslyn. "We all need our girl time."

Larinda said, "And while we've got you, we have to ask..."

Rosyln pointed at Cassie and then at Graham. "This," she declared. "It's a thing, am I right?"

Graham pulled Cassie close with an arm across her shoulders. Playing along, she leaned against him as Graham answered Roslyn with, "You'd better believe it."

A little thrill shot through her when she heard those words. *Just for now*, she scolded herself—again.

"I told you!" squealed Roslyn.

"Yes, you did!" shouted Larinda.

Poor Mike fell back from the bar a step and put up both hands. "Easy, ladies. Keep it down, now…"

"Oops," said Larinda.

Roslyn giggled. "Sorry."

"But we're just so excited!" cried Larinda. She looked at her friend. "Because it really is perfect, isn't it?"

Roslyn's head bounced up and down in agreement. She put one hand on Cassie's shoulder and the other on Graham's. "The woman who broke Jake McGeorge's heart and the guy who never gets serious. You two are meant to be."

Have we just been insulted? Cassie wondered. She didn't know for sure. She glanced at Graham. He didn't seem to know, either. As for Mike, he retreated another step and was stopped by the counter behind him.

Cassie asked cautiously, "Meant to be what, Roslyn?"

"Love, silly!" Larinda squealed and Roslyn joined in.

Mike insisted, "Ladies, *please*?"

"My bad." Larinda made an effort to look regretful. "It's just so exciting. We can hardly contain ourselves!"

"No kidding," muttered Mike.

"Tell us the truth." Now Roslyn grabbed Cassie's arm as she whisper-shouted, "Is Graham your date for Renee's wedding?"

Gently, Cassie freed her arm from Roslyn's grip. "Yes, he is."

"I knew it!" Roslyn crowed.

"Love," sighed Larinda. "One way or another, it happens for all of us. We meet our matches and suddenly we understand…"

"Understand what?" Graham asked in a worried tone.

"Everything!" declared Roslyn.

"Yes!" cried Larinda. "Exactly. That!"

From across the room, a woman called out, "'Rinda, Roz!"

Roslyn grabbed Cassie in one more hug. "So happy for you, honey. Coming!" she shrieked at her friends as she grabbed Larinda and headed back to their table.

"So much enthusiasm," Mike said with a weary sigh. "I like those two, but they tire me out."

Graham raised his glass high. "I'll drink to that."

Not much later, a group of local musicians wandered in. They set up their instruments and started playing. Graham took Cassie's hand and led her out on the floor, where they danced to one bluesy country number after another. Time kind of melted away.

They were dancing their hearts out to a cover of Chris Stapleton's "Think I'm in Love With You" when Graham swung her out and reeled her back in and murmured regretfully into her ear, "I hate to say it, but we need to go or your goats won't be happy with you…"

She almost called her mom to ask if maybe she'd deal with the goats tonight, after all. But that just wouldn't be fair. They finished the dance and Graham settled the bill.

Outside, it was still daylight, but already, the sky showed faint streaks of orange and purple as the sun descended toward the low humps of the mountains off in the distance.

The trip back to Stargazer Ranch didn't take long. Too soon, Graham was pulling up in front of the main house.

When he turned off the engine the cab seemed so quiet. "When can I call you on Sunday?" he asked.

Her silly heart lifted that he wanted to see her as soon as she got home. She wanted to see him, too.

"We'll be back by noon, but then there'll be work to catch up on. Give me a call in the evening?"

"You got it." He leaned across the console. She met him halfway. Their kiss was so sweet—and way too short. "See you Sunday," she whispered against his lips.

"Don't move," he commanded.

And then he jumped out, ran around the front of the truck—and opened her door for her.

"This is not in the least necessary," she said as he caught her hand and helped her down.

"Oh, yes it is. Because I want to kiss you again and kissing you is *always* necessary." He pulled her close. His lips touched hers and she lost herself in the moment.

"I'll miss you," he said when that kiss finally ended.

"It's only a couple of days."

"That's a couple too many—and I think I just saw the curtains move in that window to the left of the door."

She groaned. "Why am I not surprised?"

"Come on. I'll walk you up the steps."

Again, that wasn't necessary and they both knew it. Still, when he offered his arm, she took it. At the door, he gathered her close.

"How many times are you going to kiss me good-night?" she teased.

"As many as I can get away with." And he kissed her once more.

That time, when the kiss ended, she stepped back. "I hate to cut this short, but my goats are waiting."

"Tell Adelaide I miss her and I hope to see her again soon."

Two minutes later, he was back in his pickup. He waved at her as he drove away.

She'd barely gotten in the door when her mom appeared in the arch to the living room. "Did you have a nice time, honey?"

"I did, yes."

"I'm so glad. Graham is such a wonderful man."

"Yes, he is," she agreed, and made for the stairs before her mom could get rolling on the manly perfection that was Graham Callahan.

It wasn't until later, alone in her bed, with the half-moon gleaming in the window, that Cassie started feeling a little guilty about the situation with Graham. Her mom really did like him. Olive was over the moon imagining that her daughter had decided to take a chance on love again.

How was she going to feel in November when Cassie and her temporary boyfriend called it quits?

True, it wouldn't be the first time one of Cassie's relationships had curled up and died. But somehow, that it was fake in the first place had her feeling more than a little bit guilty tonight.

It was one thing to make a deal with her mom to find a date for Renee's wedding. That would only be, as both her mom and Vicky had pointed out, *just* a date for the sake of an up-front, straightforward agreement between mother and daughter.

But this thing with Graham?

Somehow, it was turning out to be so much more. He liked her and she liked him. A lot. She wanted to spend all her free time with him—and he seemed to be on the same page about that.

And the chemistry between them? Off the charts.

Too bad it wasn't going to go anywhere.

Cassie grabbed her pillow, pressed it over her face and groaned into it. The ethics of this dating arrangement were questionable at best. But she was in this now. Up to her neck—and loving it, too.

A lot.

Maybe too much…

First thing Saturday morning, Cassie, Renee, Vicky, Lucy Bernard, Chrissy Parker and Renee's yellow Lab, Buddy, piled into Olive's eight-seater SUV. The fifth bridesmaid, Miles's sister Rylee, lived in Bronco with her husband Shep Dalton now. She was there waiting for them when they arrived at Calder Creek Ranch.

The ranch and spa was everything Cassie remembered from the day she'd driven out there and booked it. Renee and her bridesmaids were pampered with hot rock massages, elaborate facials—the works.

That evening, their dinner was grilled for them out under the darkening sky. After the meal, they sat around a gorgeous rock firepit. The wide night sky was thick with stars and the fire cast a warm glow over their smiling faces.

There was a liquor cart. The guy who'd grilled their steaks to juicy perfection served them cocktails—and mocktails—of choice.

Chrissy, who would be Renee's sister-in-law once Miles and Renee exchanged their vows next Saturday, announced that marriage was the best thing that had ever happened to her.

Then Chrissy laughed. "My *second* marriage, I mean. The first one didn't turn out so well. But being married to Hayes has been worth the wait. Our life together is better than I ever dreamed it could be way back in the day when we were madly in love and barely more than kids." Chrissy and Hayes Parker had been inseparable all through high school but gone their separate ways not long after—only to reunite the previous summer.

They all raised their glasses to Chrissy and Hayes.

Renee said, "Okay, Lucy and Rylee. I want to know what I have to look forward to. Tell me your happily-ever-after stories."

Rylee went first. She and her husband, Shep, had been best friends. But last year, they'd become so much more. "It was Shep all along," she said quietly. "I just never thought we would end up as each other's forever."

Lucy said she'd never known such happiness as she had now with Noah and his toddler triplet sons. "I love Noah and those little boys. I can't wait to spend the rest of my life watching them grow up with Noah by my side."

"And we love that you're part of the family now," said Cassie.

"We do," Renee agreed. And then she demanded, "So when's the wedding?"

"Soon," Lucy promised with a secret little smile.

Now Renee turned to Cassie and Vicky, who sat side by side in Adirondack chairs. "Okay, you two. It's your turn."

Vicky knocked back another gulp of her lemon drop. "Don't even start with me, Renee. I am so happy for you—and you, and you, and you." She nodded at Chrissy, Rylee and Lucy, too. "But I am never getting married, period. Full stop."

"We shall all remember what you said here tonight," Renee remarked solemnly. "And when you finally fall, we'll say we told you so—and then congratulate you with all our hearts."

"I'll drink to that!" toasted Chrissy.

They all raised their glasses—even Vicky, who'd just been informed that she was destined to fall hopelessly in love whether she wanted to or not.

Then Renee turned to Cassie. "Okay, little sister. You and Graham Callahan. Tell all. Right now."

Cassie had known this was coming. She'd spent the last several minutes trying to decide what to say when it was her turn. But even though she should have been prepared, she wasn't.

The truth, she decided. She would tell the truth, just not *all* of it. "I like him. A lot." She was careful not to glance at Vicky, who knew far too much about the Graham situation.

Chrissy crossed her legs, plunked an elbow on her knee and braced her chin in her hand. "So then, it's serious?"

"Between me and Graham?" Cassie tried her best to appear serene. "It's early days." She should leave it at that. But then she opened her mouth and more words got out. "The truth is, we *get* each other, Graham and me. It's the strangest thing. He's exciting and fun, and yet, I feel safe with him, too." Beside her, she thought she heard Vicky scoff. At least the sound was soft enough that none of the others seemed to have noticed.

Renee was looking much too pleased with Cassie's answer. "And here I thought both you and Vicky were in the *never-going-to-happen* category when it came to love and marriage."

Cassie couldn't let that stand. "Did I just say I was going to marry him? No, I did not."

Renee was wearing her kindest, warmest smile. "But you haven't said you *won't* marry him, either."

"Well…" It was a difficult moment. She wanted to keep her agreement with Graham, but she liked and trusted these women. Lying to them just felt wrong. "I… Well, I do really like him. But you know how I feel about marriage." Her sister did know. Cassie had told Renee all about what had gone down with Butch and Craig and Jake. "I *like* men. Men are great. But the marriage thing? No. I'm just not cut out for it."

Renee gazed at her with love—and way too much understanding. "Oh, Cassie. Everything changes when the right person finally comes along."

"I don't think so, Renee. I really don't."

"Just wait," said her sister. "You'll see."

That night, they slept in the main lodge. Cassie's room had a view of the mountains and a comfortable queen-size bed. She didn't sleep that well, though. She kept thinking about the conversation around the fire pit earlier.

Her sister's words ran in a loop through her mind: *Everything changes when the right person finally comes along...*

But did it, really? Maybe for some people. Too bad Cassie wasn't one of them.

In the morning, they were served a hearty ranch breakfast before they packed up and said goodbye to their hosts. Out in the graveled parking area, they took turns hugging Rylee before she headed back to Bronco.

Cassie drove home. On the way, they discussed the wedding next Saturday. It would take place at home on Stargazer Ranch, out in the meadow where Cassie had once hoped to offer her movie nights. The minister from the Goodness & Mercy Nondenominational Church in town would officiate.

Renee sat in the back row of seats with Buddy safely tethered in the cargo area behind her. Cassie often glanced back at her in the rearview mirror.

Renee's beautiful face just glowed when she talked about her big day. She was worried, though, that they hadn't heard back from Miles's middle brother, Braden. "We invited Braden to the wedding when we first set the date. He said he'd try to make it. But he hasn't confirmed for sure and he's hard to get a hold of."

All three of the Parker brothers had a rough go of it growing up. They'd all left town at one time or another. Now both Miles and Hayes had come back to stay. Not Braden, though. He'd returned a few times since taking off—including a brief appearance last year, when their father was gravely ill—but then disappeared again after Lionel's surgery was successful. Renee really was worried he wouldn't show up for the wedding.

"Last week, Miles managed to reach him a second time," Renee said. "And again, Braden said he would *try*." She drew a slow breath. "I just hope he makes it. It means a lot to have the whole family there."

"He will be there," declared Lucy. "I just know it, and I have a sixth sense for these things."

"Right," said Renee doubtfully. But then she was smiling again. Nothing could dim her happiness, though she and Miles faced real challenges in the years ahead.

Not only did Renee need to carefully manage her diabetes, but Miles had early-onset macular degeneration caused by an injury while he was in the military. Renee's fiancé could still see, to a degree. But it wouldn't be all that long before he was completely blind. Miles had recently applied for a guide dog. He'd met all the requirements. But as of now, he was still waiting.

Cassie had never heard Miles complain about the service dog he needed but wouldn't have for months yet. Renee wasn't one to complain, either. She made her own happiness. To Cassie, it seemed that both Renee and Miles viewed the difficulties they confronted as simply a part of life. They found happiness in knowing that they would be facing all their challenges together.

From the seat behind Cassie, Vicky announced, "We all know how I feel about love and marriage—but Renee, if any couple has a chance to make it work, you and Miles are it."

"Thank you, Victoria," Renee said fondly.

"It's only the truth."

"Yes, it is," declared Lucy, who sat in the passenger seat next to Cassie.

Renee's glance shifted to Cassie in the mirror. "You're too quiet…"

Cassie's eyes had misted over. She sent her sister a giant smile. "I'm just so happy for you," she said.

Renee had tears in her eyes, too. She seemed about to reply. But in the end, she only gave Cassie a quick nod and returned her smile. They left it at that.

At a little after eight that night, Cassie sat on a stool in the goat shed with one of her best milk producers up on the milking stand. Her phone rang. It was Graham.

She answered on speaker, set the phone under her stool and kept right on milking. "Hi."

"You home?"

She smiled at the sound of his voice. She'd missed him. Maybe more than she should have…

"Cassie? You there?"

"Right here—and yeah. I'm home."

The doe Cassie was milking lifted her head from the feed bucket long enough to let out a bleat.

"I hear a goat," Graham said.

"It's milking time. Jolene says hi."

He chuckled—and Cassie found herself grinning like a fool again. "Which one is she?" he asked.

"I doubt you've met her yet. She's a full-grown doe who's produced six beautiful kids so far. She's not as adventurous as Adelaide, mostly stays in the pen where she belongs. I'll be sure to introduce you one of these days."

"Good. Adelaide loves me. I'm betting Jolene will, too."

"Don't count on it. Jolene's very self-possessed. You might have trouble winning her over." Again, Jolene lifted her head in the stanchion and let out a long bleat.

Graham asked, "That was Jolene, right?"

"So?"

"Well, you heard what she said, didn't you? She loves me already. All your goats are bound to love me, just you wait and see."

Cassie kept milking. "I'm very busy here." She was trying hard to sound stern. "Was there something you needed?"

"Yeah." His voice had gone low and deliciously rough. "I missed you. It's been three whole days. That's a lifetime as far as I'm concerned."

"What you're saying is that we need to get out and be seen together, right?" Was she taunting him?

Maybe.

A little.

"Yes, we do." The guy didn't miss a beat. "It's important. For the sake of my campaign."

"Right. *So* important…"

"We should get together right away. Alone. To talk about…our plans. How about tonight? Tonight really works for me. It just so happens I'm free."

She stopped milking. Jolene shifted on the stand.

Cassie shook herself and got back to the job again. "You want me to drive over to your place once I've milked all my goats?"

"No way. That's asking too much. I'll come pick you up."

She opened her mouth to say she couldn't. "When?" popped out.

"As soon as you're done with the goats."

She should be finished with the milking in about half an hour. "An hour," she said. After all, she needed to freshen up a bit.

"See you then."

Graham got there fifteen minutes early. Was he eager?

Damn straight. This thing between them was hot as a grass fire burning up the high plains.

Plus, it only seemed right to say hi to Olive and Mr. Trent if they were home. Cassie came downstairs all fresh and pink-cheeked in a red shirt and faded Wranglers as he and Olive were chatting in the front hall.

"I'll be back before midnight," Cassie promised, and kissed her mom's cheek.

"Oh, now," said Olive, beaming. "You two have fun."

"We will," Graham replied with enthusiasm and pulled Cassie out the front door.

It was a twenty-minute drive to his house. He made it in record time.

"That was fast," she said. "We must have a lot of important stuff to talk about."

"You have no idea…"

A minute later, they were running up the front steps hand-in-hand.

Izzy was waiting. Crouching on the porch, Cassie told

the wriggling dog how happy she was to see her. Izzy rolled to her back, her tongue lolling out. That dog was shameless. She whined in ecstasy as Cassie scratched her belly.

At last, Cassie allowed him to usher her inside. He took her hand and pulled her straight to his room. Once he had her past the threshold, he swung the door shut. Cassie smiled up at him, her big eyes low and full of heat.

"Now," he said. "Where were we?"

"The campaign," she replied dreamily. "We were going to talk about—"

"Later for that."

She laughed as he pulled her in good and close again. She smelled so fresh and sweet and her mouth was right there...

He swooped down and claimed it. She made the sexiest, hungriest little sound low in her throat. He drank that sound right down. As he kissed her, he started undressing her.

She took the hint and got busy helping him out of his shirt.

They left a trail of clothing on the floor as they kissed their way over to the bed. He had his hands in her hair and his mouth all over her.

By then, both of them were naked as the day they were born. She took his face between her palms and pretended to scowl at him. "What about all this talking we just *have* to do?"

By way of an answer, he hauled her close and kissed her some more. She kissed him back, hard and sweet and so, so deep. As for the feel of her bare body pressed close against him...

Paradise.

When they fell across the bed, he was already reaching for the nightstand drawer. He had a condom out and on in seconds flat.

And then he was rolling her under him—or maybe she was pulling him on top of her. He hardly knew who was initiating what. Not that it mattered. However it had happened, he was suddenly braced up on his arms with his hips cradled between her open thighs.

"Cassie…" Her name on his lips was a desperate plea.

"Yes!" Her eyes locked with his, she reached down between them. Careful of the condom, she guided him into her welcoming heat. A tender cry escaped her as she wrapped those strong legs around him and hooked her ankles at the small of his back.

Nothing, he thought in a shattered sort of way. *Nothing in the world has ever felt this good.* He bent close and took her lips again. She tasted of everything he'd been missing so desperately since Thursday.

He kissed her and went on kissing her. At first, except for his mouth moving on hers, they were still. But that couldn't last. Needing to take them higher, he began to rock against her slowly. But then he just had to move faster. Things got intense. They moved together in heated waves.

The everyday world spun away, and he wished that this magic might go on forever, that it could be just him and Cassie, here on his big log bed, moving together from now into eternity, every nerve ending alive with heat and need and urgency.

Too soon, she cried his name. He felt her body pulsing around him. He lost it then, too. Together, they soared over the edge of the world.

* * *

Limp with satisfaction, Cassie almost drifted off. Her eyes were drooping. She knew she wouldn't be awake for long. Graham dropped a kiss on her shoulder and left the bed.

But then he was back. He stretched out beside her and pulled her into his lean, hard arms.

"I should go," she whispered, snuggling closer. "If we fall asleep, I'll end up here all night."

"What a great idea." His lips brushed her tangled hair. "You should stay."

"Not happening." She forced her eyelids open and braced her hands on his chest, which was warm and hard and dusted with crisp dark hair.

He gave her that devilish smile of his. The man was incorrigible, and she liked that about him way too much.

She blinked up at him. "Ready to talk about the campaign?"

He kissed the end of her nose. "Not now. Maybe tomorrow...?"

She widened her eyes and teased, "I thought it was urgent, that we *had* to discuss the campaign tonight."

He gave a low, rough chuckle. "Not as urgent as having your undivided attention while I do shocking things to your beautiful body."

Playfully, she shoved at his gorgeous chest. "You lured me here under false pretenses."

"Oh, you bet I did." He caught a lock of her hair and wrapped it around his finger. "Because I like this—you and me, here in my bed. I like it a lot. And I want you stay—at least for a while." He gave her a look that made her heart ache in the sweetest, most tender way. "Please, Cassie. Stay..."

Her poor heart melted. "I can't be allowed to drop off to sleep."

"Fair enough."

"I need to get going in the next hour—two at the most."

"You got it." He retreated to the other pillow. She missed him immediately, but somehow kept herself from pulling him back into her hungry arms.

Instead, she turned on her side to face him. "So then, how do you propose to make sure I stay awake?"

A smoking-hot smile lit up his handsome face. He reached for her again.

She laughed and showed him the flat of her hand. "You are insatiable."

He faked a frown. "That's a mighty big word, young lady."

"You are also incorrigible."

He leaned in closer. "What can I tell you? Oh, yes I am."

She lifted up enough to kiss him hard and quick. Because she did want him. Again.

And why not? They could make it fast and then, right afterward, she would get up and go.

He brushed a finger along her cheek. His touch stirred sparks in its wake. "You're so much fun, Cassie. I love that about you. I love a lot of things about you..." His mouth met hers in a long, lazy kiss.

She wanted to go on doing this forever—kissing him, losing herself in the thrill of his touch.

But beyond the powerful physical connection she had with him, she wanted...more. Recently, she'd started coming to grips with that, with her longing to know everything about him—his history, his heartaches, what made him tick.

Where had this growing hunger to know him more deeply come from?

Who cares? she asked herself and realized she didn't give a hoot why she felt this way. She liked him and she wanted to understand him. It didn't have to be a big deal.

She pulled back. "So here's the thing. The truth is, I was thinking that I do want to know your story…"

His dark eyebrows drew together. "My story of…?"

Suddenly, her throat was tight. She put her hand to her mouth and gave a nervous little cough. "Your past loves—you know, what happened with them that made you decide not to go there again."

He blinked. "You're serious?"

"I am. I want to know about the women in your life. I want to know why those relationships didn't work out and how you ended up deciding you would never get married."

Chapter Nine

Graham didn't want to go there.

Not now. Not anymore. A week ago, he wouldn't have minded laying it all out there.

But now?

No. Just no. He didn't want to tell her about Serena, about what a damn blind fool he'd been.

But why not? he kept asking himself. The story was what it was, and previously, he'd been completely willing to give her the gory details. When he'd offered to tell her everything on that first night he took her to Castillo's, he would have done so without batting an eye.

Yet now, somehow...

It felt wrong. Scary. Like he'd be showing her too much, revealing stuff she just didn't need to know.

After all, he reasoned, they only went so far as a couple—because they weren't a couple, not really. They were helping each other out, *pretending* to be a couple—and somehow, the pretending had turned into...more.

Too much more?

Of course not. This, with her, was so good. Fun and sexy, easy. Right. Getting into past heartbreak just seemed dangerous now.

And what good would it do for either of them to go digging up the betrayals of the past?

Nope. Not going there.

He opened his mouth to say so—but before he said a word, she suggested very gently, "How about if I go first?"

He should shut this subject down right now. Remind her that they were together only until after the election, that he loved being with her, but getting in too deep was a bad idea. That there needed to be boundaries, that they should keep things in perspective.

But he couldn't do it. Because the chances were very real that refusing to talk about his past now would mess up the good thing they had going on. She would pull away.

He wasn't ready to lose her. Not yet. He liked her. He liked everything about her, and he couldn't bear the thought of losing her so soon.

Plus, well, he wanted to hear *her* story. And if the price for learning her secrets was sharing the stuff he no longer had any desire to talk about, well, he would pay that price.

"Okay then…" Catching her fingers, he brought them to his lips for a quick, light kiss. "Tell me everything."

"You sure?"

"I am."

"All right." She braced her elbow on the pillow and her cheek on her hand. "First you should know that as a kid, growing up, I was your total tomboy. I loved horses and the great outdoors and I had zero interest in girlie things…"

"I'm not the least surprised." He wanted to reach for her, pull her into his arms again, kiss her senseless—and then kiss her some more.

But somehow he managed to keep his hands to himself.

She said, "Then, in high school, I met Butch Bixby."

"The football player?"

"That's the one."

Bixby had been a big deal, Graham remembered, the star quarterback for the Tenacity Titans. He'd been a star at the University of Colorado, too. And after that, he'd gone pro. The way Graham remembered it, Bixby's professional career never really took off.

That Cassie had dated the guy? That was news to him. But he'd been living in Seattle when she was in high school. At that time, he hadn't had much interest in what went on in his hometown.

"I fell hard for Butch," Cassie said. "He was everything to me. You wouldn't have recognized me then. I was suddenly the girliest girl at Tenacity High. Senior year, Butch and I were the king and queen of both Homecoming and prom. Butch got a football scholarship to Colorado and I could not wait to marry him and have his babies."

Graham realized he hated Butch Bixby. A lot. "What did he do to you?"

She looked at him patiently. "It's not what you think. Butch wanted me to go with him to Colorado."

"So he was a stand-up guy, is that what you're telling me?"

"Yeah. He was, as a matter of fact. But by graduation, I'd begun to realize that Butch and I didn't agree about the most important things."

"Like…?"

"Well, I'd always wanted to go to State to study ranch management, then to come back home and spend my life on Stargazer Ranch. Butch just didn't get why I suddenly had plans of my own.

"He said I didn't need to go to college, and I wouldn't

be living on the family ranch because I was going to be his wife and follow him wherever his career took him."

"Whoa. Butch really thought he ran the show, didn't he?"

"Yes, he did. And at first, I just went along with everything he said. But by the end of Senior year, I'd begun to feel resentful that he could so easily dismiss what mattered to me."

"So you broke it off with him?"

She shook her head. "I had loved him since freshman year. I kept telling myself we would somehow work it out. He popped the question before he went off to Colorado. He wanted me to marry him that summer and go with him to Boulder."

"Tell me you said no."

"Not outright. I balked, though. I just couldn't do it. I said I needed time to think it over. Butch wasn't happy, but he agreed to give me the summer at home to make up my mind."

"So...in the end, you did say no."

Her eyes were far away, lost in the past. "I'd spent four years in love with Butch. I thought Butch was everything. I was planning our wedding when I was sixteen. But by the end of the summer after senior year, I had to accept that Butch and me, we didn't want the same things. I broke it off."

"Wow. How did Butch take that?"

"He was hurt. But he was also done. I mean, he was Butch Bixby and he wasn't going to be hanging around Tenacity trying to convince a hometown girl that she was making the biggest mistake of her life. He went to Colorado and never looked back."

"And you went to Montana State?"

"I did. I went to State and met Craig James, an Education major from Idaho. Craig was a good guy, he really was. After college, he planned to go back home to Idaho Falls to teach high school English…"

In their senior year at State, Craig had proposed—and Cassie balked again. "I love Tenacity," she said. "It's my home. And I love the family ranch and I never want to live anywhere else. I explained all that to Craig. He said he had his dream, a dream that really mattered. He said he wanted me to live that dream with him. Well, as I had already told him, I had my own dream."

"You broke it off with Craig."

"Oh, yes I did."

Graham saw the pattern. "Neither Bixby nor Craig took what *you* wanted into consideration."

She grinned. "That's right. I saw it as their problem. But then along came Jake McGeorge…"

"The famous local saddlemaker."

"Used to be local," she corrected kind of glumly.

After Cassie graduated from Montana State, she'd returned to Tenacity. "For a year or so, I only dated casually. But then, four years ago, I started going out with Jake. I really liked him. Jake's a great guy, and he was more than willing to build a house on the family ranch and move in with me there. He said whatever I wanted, that was okay with him. Three years ago, he bought a beautiful diamond ring and got down on one knee to propose."

"And you said no again?"

"I did. I liked him so much, but when it came to promising forever…no. I couldn't do it. I tried to let him down easy, but Jake took it real hard. He closed up his shop and left town for good. Everyone was shocked that I sent a man like Jake packing. I was shocked, too."

"Because you realized you didn't love him?"

"Exactly. I didn't love him. Jake's a fine man, a good guy. I admired him. He should have been the one. He was willing to do whatever he had to do, whatever *I* needed him to do to make it work between us." She frowned in a thoughtful way. "But there was no making it work because *I* am the problem."

"Cassie..." He wanted to comfort her and started to reach out.

She shook her head. "Just let me finish."

He kept his hands to himself. "Go on."

"That's why I'm done," she said. "I'm finished with the love thing. I'm not breaking another good man's heart, you know? I'm just fine on my own—more than fine. Love and marriage? They're just not for me."

He wasn't sure what to say now.

And she knew it. "Speechless, huh? You thought I was going to tell you about the men who did *me* wrong. You never guessed that I'm the bad guy in my own story."

"Cassie. You're not the bad guy. Someday you'll meet someone who—"

"Stop. Please. I don't need reassurance. I don't need a pep talk. I like my life just the way it is. I mean, somebody has to be the fun, eccentric auntie with a bunch of cute cats—or in my case, adorable goats. That'll be me, teaching my nephews and nieces how to rope, ride and milk the goats."

He wasn't sure what to say. "I get what you're telling me. You don't want to hurt another good man."

"Exactly. And I won't. I'm not leading anyone on ever again. I'm not wasting any man's time. I'm always going to make it crystal clear from the first that if you're looking for a wife, don't look at me." She smiled then, a real smile. "So that's it. You know where I stand and why."

"Come here," he said.

She narrowed her eyes at him. "Why?"

"Please..." He reached out again. This time, she allowed him to pull her close. She sighed as their lips met. He drank in the soft sound.

When she lifted away again, he said, "I still don't see how you're the bad guy, not with Butch, Craig *or* Jake."

"I don't think I'm the bad guy. I'm just not a coupling-up sort of person. I'm happy with my life as it is."

He longed to argue with her, to explain to her why she really shouldn't turn her back on love.

But come on. How was it his place to do that?

She didn't need some guy like him mansplaining why she should give love another chance—one of these days with someone other than him.

And why was it that when he thought of her with those other guys, he kind of felt like putting his fist through a wall?

She was watching him. He knew it was his turn to do the talking, and he really wanted to wiggle out of it somehow.

Her lips curved in a tiny smile then. "Tell you what. Enough for one night. I've told you mine. We'll save yours for some other time." She started to throw back the covers.

He caught her hand. "Uh-uh. Fair is fair."

She studied his face. "You sure?"

No. He wasn't the least sure. He didn't want to tell her what a damn fool he'd been.

But better a fool than a stone coward. "I'm sure."

"Okay, then..." She propped her pillow against the headboard and sat back against it. "Fire away."

He sat up beside her. "You know that I went to the University of Washington in Seattle…" At her nod, he continued, "My first day there, I met my best friend. His name is Kevin Masters. He was an Econ major, same as me, from a Wyoming ranching family."

"So you and Kevin have a lot in common."

"That's right. We got assigned to share a dorm room freshman year, and right away we hit it off. My original plan was to get my four-year degree and come back home. But then senior year, I met Serena Leverson. She was smart and funny and very nice to look at."

Cassie was watching his face. "You fell hard."

"I did, yeah. I knew by our second date that Serena was the one. She was a Seattle girl through and through, and she made it crystal clear she wouldn't be moving to the wilds of Montana. I just wanted to be wherever she was. We decided I would stay right there at UW and get my MBA.

"And that's how, at twenty-four, with an MBA in Economics, I went to work as a financial analyst for a large Seattle construction firm. My buddy, Kevin, stayed in Seattle, too. As for Serena and me, we were still together and going strong. Two years later, Serena said yes."

"You've been *married*?" She blinked in obvious disbelief.

He gave her a wry smile. "Who's telling this story?"

She put her hand to her mouth. "Sorry. Continue…"

He did, reluctantly. "Serena and I were both twenty-seven on the day of our wedding." He watched, hiding a bleak smile, as Cassie pressed her lips together to keep from interrupting again. He laid it out there. "It's the oldest story in the book. She left me standing at the altar."

"Oh, no…" Cassie said the two words in a forlorn little whisper.

"Oh, yeah. She left me standing at the altar to run off with my best friend—and best man—Kevin."

Cassie gasped.

He went on, "I was pretty sure on my supposed wedding day that she'd run away with Kevin."

"Because he didn't show up at the church, either…"

"That's right. I found out for certain a couple of days later when she finally got around to emailing me. Serena wrote that she was so sorry but she just hadn't been able to go through with marrying me. That she would have been miserable and I would, too. Because, as it turned out, she and Kevin had been having an affair since Kevin and I were in grad school."

Cassie whispered, "No…"

"Oh, yeah. She wrote that she'd tried over and over to break it off with my best friend. But finally, on the night before our wedding, she realized why she couldn't make herself end it with Kevin. It was because he was the one she really loved."

Cassie just looked at him for the longest time. Finally, she said, "I am so sorry, Graham."

"Don't be. I was a fool."

"No. Uh-uh." Her beautiful eyes flashed blue fire. "You were truehearted. You were the good guy. You loved her and you were not in any way a fool. You are not the one to blame in that story. Don't you dare go beating up on yourself for believing in your girl and trusting your best friend."

He shut his eyes and shook his head. "Yeah, well. Now you know—and since Serena, there have been several other women. But I always keep things casual, which you already know. I never let anyone get too close."

"Hey." She waited until he looked at her again before asking, "Are you okay?"

He gave a humorless laugh. "Not really. Do you want the truth?"

"Yes, I do."

"I don't want to talk about this anymore." Because telling her that story made him feel like he'd taken a cheese grater to his own heart.

"I understand," she softly replied.

He didn't know what to say next. For an awkward string of seconds, they simply stared at each other.

Finally, she spoke again. "I should probably go home."

"Yeah. All right. I'll take you home…"

She swung her feet to the rug and crouched to grab her underwear. He stared at the gorgeous curves of her backside. With a quick, questioning glance at him over her shoulder, she rose and stepped into her panties. He longed to pull her back into the bed with him, to let the sweet reality of holding her wipe out all the ugly memories of the past.

Instead, he said roughly, "Come out and knock on doors with me Tuesday?"

"I'm in." Her smile made everything better.

Graham picked her up at two-thirty Tuesday afternoon. They each took a stack of the newest brochure he'd put together and went door-to-door separately to talk to people about why they should elect him mayor.

Afterward, at his place, he grilled the trout he'd caught that day in Callahan Creek. Neither of them brought up the things they'd revealed to each other Sunday night. Instead, they discussed the campaign and agreed it was going well.

People were really interested in the mayoral race. Folks wanted a fresh start for the town and someone new at the helm, someone honest, with a real plan to turn things around.

Before he took her home, they spent two beautiful hours in his bed. He kept waiting for her to mention the things they'd told each other on Sunday night.

She never said a word. He appreciated that she let it be. He didn't want to go there again.

Wednesday, he drove to Bronco to pick up a couple of tractor parts he couldn't get there in town. Back at home, he put the parts in the tractor shed and went into the house, thinking he would grab a quick bite to eat before trying to get the tractor running again.

He found water trickling across the kitchen floor.

A seal had broken on one of the pipes under the sink. It took him four hours to fix it, including two trips into town, where he visited both Strom and Son Feed and Farm Supply *and* Tenacity Feed and Seed to find the right parts.

At eight that night, as he devoured a solitary dinner of leftovers he'd scrounged from the fridge, he decided it was too late to give Cassie a call. Plus, he was still feeling kind of raw after what he'd told her Sunday night. He didn't think she'd bring it up. She hadn't said a word the night before.

But hey, a little distance couldn't hurt.

He went to bed alone and wished she was there and reminded himself that he really needed to keep things in perspective. Cassie was amazing. But come on. They couldn't go spending every spare moment together.

Thursday, he called her. She didn't pick up, so he left a message. "Hey. Call me when you get a chance..."

By the time she got back to him it was after nine that night. As it turned out, she'd spent the day and evening dealing with last-minute preparations for her sister's wedding. She reminded him that Friday was the rehearsal and the dinner afterward. He wasn't in the wedding party, so he wouldn't be seeing her that day, either.

Truth was, he missed her. A lot.

Which was fine, he told himself. Understandable. They had a good thing going on and he wanted to lay claim to every minute he could get with her. Each day without her was a day he wished he'd spent with her.

Was he becoming too attached? Definitely.

And he could not wait for Saturday when he would be her date for her sister's wedding.

On Saturday morning, Cassie hit the ground running. Yes, her sister was getting married today. But first, eggs needed gathering and goats needed milking.

She finished the usual chores in record time, slammed down a quick breakfast and then got busy with all the things that had to be done before the big event.

The hours flew by...

Cassie kept thinking she needed to check in with Renee, but there was never a spare moment to get her sister alone. By late afternoon, all the bridesmaids were getting ready in Cassie's room. The bride had the large upstairs bathroom to herself.

Cassie saw her chance and took it. "Back in a sec," she said to the others. "I'm just going to check on Renee."

"Go for it," Chrissy replied. Lucy nodded and Vicky answered with a shrug. Rylee simply smiled.

Cassie left them in her bedroom and zipped across the upstairs hall to tap on the bathroom door.

"It's open," Renee called from inside.

Cassie poked her head in. "How're you doing?"

Renee, with Buddy snoozing at her feet, sat at the vanity table they'd carried in there that morning from their mother's room. "Just about ready. Come on in."

Cassie entered the room, shut the door and leaned back against it. "You look amazing."

Renee tipped her head from one side to the other as she studied her reflection in the trifold mirror. Her hair flowed loose on her shoulders and her smooth skin glowed against the delicate ivory lace of her dress. Their eyes met in the mirror. Renee frowned.

"What's wrong?" Cassie went to her.

His tail bumping the floor, Buddy glanced up. The dog seemed completely relaxed. If Renee's blood sugar was out of whack, he would be on alert.

But just to be sure, Cassie asked, "Are you feeling okay?"

Renee smiled then. "Yes. I feel great."

"Got those glucose tablets handy?"

Renee nodded and patted the almost-invisible pocket she'd sewn into the waistband of her wedding dress. "Right here whenever I need them." Renee gave her a smile.

Despite all Renee's reassurances, Cassie thought she saw apprehension in her sister's big blue eyes. "*Something's* wrong..."

Renee's bright smile dimmed a bit. "Yeah, well..."

"Tell me."

"I'm just a little worried, that's all."

"About...?"

"We still don't know whether Braden's coming or not."

"You're kidding me."

"Nope."

"What is the matter with that guy?"

"Hey." Renee sighed. "He's a Parker. They have issues."

Lionel Parker, Miles's dad, had always been a difficult man to deal with. He'd been hard on all three of his sons while they were growing up. From what Cassie had heard, at least Lionel had been easier on Rylee, his only daughter. Apparently, the Parker patriarch was one of those misguided men who thought tough love would serve the boys well later in life.

Cassie asked, "So the last you heard from Braden, he was still saying he would *try* to make it."

"That's about the size of it, yeah."

"If he promised to try to come, I'm sure he'll be here," Cassie said with more confidence than she actually felt.

Renee wasn't fooled. "And you know this, how?"

Cassie put on her most serene and confident expression. "Trust me."

Renee laughed then. "I do trust you. I'm just afraid you're wrong." On the floor, her dog lifted his golden head and yawned.

"See? Buddy's not worried, either." Cassie bent to kiss her sister's cheek. "Have faith."

"Do I have a choice?"

"Nope. I'm the maid of honor and I make the rules here."

"Sure you do—and on a happier note..." Renee was grinning now—a real grin. "You and Graham Callahan are looking very cozy lately."

Not as cozy as we used to be, she thought. Lately, he seemed to be pulling away a little—which she did understand. Neither of them could afford to get too attached, after all.

And her sister was watching her much too closely. Cassie put on an easy smile. "He's a good guy and I like him."

"I noticed."

"And I think he would make a great mayor. So we're enjoying each other's company and I'm helping him out with his campaign." Okay, she did feel a bit guilty that she'd yet to tell her sister that she and Graham weren't exactly what they seemed to be. She needed to get honest and she knew it. But telling Renee the real situation right now, explaining that she'd made a deal with Graham to be his fake girlfriend...

Uh-uh. Not on her sister's wedding day.

Renee caught Cassie's hand. "Hey. I'm excited that you've found someone special. I really am. I mean, it's been a while."

"Didn't I just explain that it's not like that between me and Graham? You know very well that I'm not getting serious with any guy, not after what I did to Jake."

"I do know. But you *are* allowed to change your mind. Cassie, you went into the relationship with Jake in good faith. And when he proposed and you just weren't feeling it, what else could you do but turn him down as gently as possible?"

"But I honestly thought I would marry him. We had long talks, Jake and me. We agreed that we both wanted marriage and a family. So I did lead him on. I'm sure if you asked Jake, he would say I misled him and then I dumped him when he asked me to marry him."

"I don't have to ask Jake. I know what happened. You were honest and kind and he didn't take it well."

"Thank you. I love that you see it that way."

"I see it that way because that's how it was," Renee insisted.

Cassie decided not to argue the point further. "Truly, Graham and I are not serious about each other." Why did that feel like a lie as she said it? It wasn't a lie. They *weren't* serious. They were just for now and having fun.

"Oh, come on," said Renee. "I see how you two look at each other. I have a really good feeling about what you and Graham have together."

Cassie hated lying to her sister. She had to grit her teeth to keep from spilling the real story right then and there.

Later, she reminded herself yet again. *Now is not the time.*

Graham, in a white dress shirt, his best felt hat, a two-button jacket and alligator boots buffed to a high shine, arrived at Stargazer Ranch in time to get a pretty good seat in the third row of folding chairs out in the big green meadow well away from the goat pen, but not far from the red barn.

Under a spreading hackberry tree about thirty feet from where the guests were seated, the Trents had put up one of those portable dance floors. Party lights were strung in the branches above it. Even with the August sun shining brightly in the cloudless sky, the lights gave off a pretty glow.

On the dance floor, a string quartet of local musicians played instrumental versions of romantic country songs as Miles's parents and then Cassie's dad and mom were escorted to their seats.

A few minutes later, the minister of Goodness & Mercy Nondenominational Church stepped behind the podium that faced the rows of chairs. A hush fell over the guests as Miles Parker, his brother Hayes and Miles's scruffy little rescue dog, Jasper, took their places to the right of the minister. The Parker brothers stood side-by-side. The little dog, panting happily, his pink tongue hanging out of the side of his mouth, sat down between them. Just looking at that dog had Graham grinning. Cassie had mentioned Jasper once or twice and said how cute he was. She'd been right.

The wedding march began. Renee's bridesmaids came slowly forward and lined up to the left of the minister. The bridesmaids all wore simple, flowing dresses and carried small wildflower bouquets. Cassie was the prettiest, hands down—and yeah, Graham might have been just a tad prejudiced on that point.

But then again, no. She was beautiful in that effortless, sunny way of hers. No other woman could even compare. Not in Graham's opinion, anyway.

Next, three little ring bearers in Western-style tuxedos appeared—they were Cassie's brother Noah's triplet sons. The first boy wore dark glasses and a sign around his neck that declared him Ring Security. The other two held small, carved wooden boxes. Noah walked beside them, herding them, keeping the boys on track as they toddled along.

An audible sigh went up from the rows of folding chairs when the bride appeared. She wore flowing white lace and she carried an armful of summer flowers. A yellow Labrador retriever trotting proudly at her side.

Renee and the yellow Lab joined the groom and his small, scruffy mutt. The string quartet fell silent for the vows, which were simple and straightforward. Renee and

Miles promised to love, honor and cherish each other for the rest of their lives.

When the minister said, "You may kiss your bride," a hush settled over the crowd.

Miles Parker gently lifted Renee's veil and smoothed it back. The silence from the guests was downright reverent as Miles took his wife in his arms.

After the ceremony, they all lined up to shake the hands of the bride, the groom and both sets of parents. Graham congratulated Miles and wished Renee much happiness. He chatted briefly with the Parker parents and with the Trents. Then he went looking for Cassie.

He spotted her over by the dance floor. She was talking with Mrs. Shanahan, who taught music at Tenacity High and had played the cello in the string quartet earlier. When Cassie caught sight of him watching her, she gave Mrs. Shanahan a quick hug and then headed his way. He met her halfway.

"Beautiful ceremony," he said when they stood close together. He leaned even closer. "Almost as beautiful as the maid of honor."

"Thank you. But have you *seen* my sister? No one can compare."

He didn't argue. The bride was lovely, after all.

The Trents had set up long tables right there in the meadow under the wide Montana sky. The guests sat down to a feast of brisket, baked beans, corn bread and potato salad. The food was great, the weather was beautiful and the newlyweds were blissfully happy together.

Graham enjoyed himself. After the meal, he and Cassie chatted with Hayes Parker and his wife, Chrissy.

Victoria Woodson wandered over. She and Cassie went

off together. He made the rounds, visiting with people he'd known all his life.

Cassie reappeared at his side as he was touching base with Mel Hastings who owned the tractor store in town. She slipped her arm in his, leaned close and whispered, "Look at you. Building your constituency one wedding guest at a time."

"Hardly. Mel and I were discussing the weather, as a matter of fact."

"Sounds riveting."

"Oh, you'd better believe it." Graham wanted to wrap her up in his arms and kiss her—a long, hot, hungry kiss, after which he would carry her off somewhere private. Somewhere with a bed.

But that wasn't to be. Not right now, anyway. There was still dancing and toasts, cake-cutting and bouquet-throwing to get through.

Victoria Woodson appeared again at Cassie's side. She seemed to be giving Graham the evil eye, which made him wonder what, exactly, he'd done wrong.

But then, he knew things weren't that great for Victoria right now, what with the scandal surrounding her dad and mom. He decided not to let her attitude get to him.

As the night came on, a local band set up their instruments next to the dance floor. Under the party lights, the bride and groom shared their first dance as a married couple.

Soon, other couples were swaying beneath the lights.

Graham leaned close to Cassie and whispered, "Dance with me."

She tipped her sweet face up to him, her eyes alight, her mouth curving in a glorious smile. "Yes."

A few feet away, Victoria continued to scowl. But then

Cassie put her hand in his and he led her to the dance floor. They had fun through a couple of fast songs.

And then, at last, there was a slow one. The perfect slow one—Thomas Rhett's "Die a Happy Man." Graham pulled her close and she fit so right. They moved like they had those nights at the Social Club—like they'd been dancing together all of their lives. And when she looked up at him through those beautiful eyes, well...

He didn't even stop to think that he might be taking it too far, getting too intimate right out there in public. There was only Cassie, so slim and strong in his arms, and his heart that was aching to somehow bust through the cage of his ribs to get to her.

Her soft mouth was right there, tipped up to him.

He claimed it.

The music, the night, the people all around them... Poof! Gone.

It was just the two of them, Graham and Cassie, swaying together, kissing slow and sweet. He didn't want to stop, not ever.

He opened his eyes reluctantly to find her watching him. Slowly, he lifted his head, breaking the kiss. She continued to stare up at him, dreamy eyed. He could go on like this forever, swaying to the music, holding Cassie in his arms.

But too soon, the song ended. And in the moment before the next song began, he heard someone shout, "It's Braden! Braden Parker..."

Cassie blinked up at him as though startled from a dream. "Braden's here?"

"Let's find out." He pulled her toward the edge of the dance floor.

But she hung back. "Graham, look!"

He spotted Braden then. The long-lost Parker brother was walking slowly across the meadow from the road. Looking somewhat grim and yet very determined, Braden matched his pace to that of the adorable little girl who had hold of his hand.

Over by the tables, Rylee Dalton let out a happy cry at the sight of her long-lost brother. "Braden! You came!"

"You bet I did!" Braden called back. Rylee took off running to meet him, every other Parker in attendance falling in behind her. Braden paused to swing the child up into his arms. "And guess what?" he added, smiling now. "I've got someone special for you to meet. This is Delilah, my little girl!"

Chapter Ten

"I need to head home soon…" Happily breathless and thoroughly satisfied, Cassie fell back on the pillow and stared up at the log ceiling overhead. They were at Graham's house and had been for a couple of hours—a couple of very passionate hours.

After Braden Parker's arrival and the surprise introduction of his daughter, Delilah, to the rest of the Parker family, there had been more to come, including the cake cutting and an endless chain of toasts to the bride and groom. Next came the bouquet throwing. Cassie had to duck when Renee sent that thing flying straight for her. Luckily Lucy had been standing right behind her and caught it with a happy laugh.

Finally, after midnight, Cassie had pulled her sister aside.

"Listen, Renee," she'd said hesitantly. "I was wondering if—"

"Go." Renee had that look in her eye. She knew exactly where Cassie was going. "Have fun."

"You're sure?"

"Of course."

"Mom won't be happy that I just took off."

Renee had shrugged. "I'll handle Mom."

So Cassie and Graham had gone to his house.

Now she rolled her head on the pillow to meet his fine dark eyes. "It's almost three and I have to be up at—"

He silenced her with a kiss, one that cleared her brain of all rational thought. Then he said, "Stay a little longer. When I drive you home, I'll stick around and help with putting things away after the party last night."

"You really don't have to—"

"But I want to." He kissed the space between her eyebrows.

"Well." She made a big show of pretending to think it over. "This bed *is* very comfortable…"

"Stay. I'll take you home at dawn. And when we get there, you can count on me to pitch in with cleanup, to milk the goats, whatever. I'll help with whatever needs doing."

"You really are the best fake boyfriend ever."

"I try…" He fell back to his own pillow.

After a moment of silence, she let out a soft sigh. "I can't believe Braden Parker's got a five-year-old daughter—Delilah. I love that name. And she looks just like him, same smile, same blue eyes and light brown hair…"

"Spitting image, that's for sure."

"No sign of Delilah's mom, though." Cassie frowned. "What's the story with that, I wonder?"

"You know how fast news travels in this town. We'll find out everything soon enough."

"You think maybe he and that little girl are home to stay?" she asked.

"Who knows?" Graham replied. "But that would be something, all three of Lionel Parker's sons back in town at last."

Hayes Parker had left right after high school. Everyone said he would never come home. Then Braden went off on his own and only showed up in Tenacity once in a blue moon. And then Miles had joined the service. Rylee had stayed closer to home. She'd moved to Bronco an hour and a half away. In Bronco, she and her lifelong friend Shep Dalton had become *more* than friends and made good on their childhood promise to marry by thirty.

"The Parker family, reunited," Cassie said with a sigh. "I think that's beautiful."

He scooted close to her again and nuzzled her ear. "I think *you're* beautiful."

She laid her hand on his warm, hard chest with its perfect smattering of crisp dark hair. "You're a smooth talker, Graham Callahan."

"Kiss me," he said. "That'll shut me up."

She didn't argue, just lifted her eager mouth to his.

As promised, Graham drove Cassie home at dawn. She reminded him again that he didn't have to stay.

But he wanted to stay. He hung around all morning, helping to load the borrowed tables and chairs into the beds of various pickups so the owners could take them home. He took down party lights and helped disassemble the dance floor.

At noon, as he was about to go, Olive came trotting out of the house, grabbed his arm and pulled him inside to share the afternoon meal. There were five of them around the table—Olive, Christopher, Cassie, Ryder and Graham. Noah and his family were at his place. As for the newlyweds, they'd packed up their gear and their dogs and headed off for a five-day honeymoon at a rustic cabin in Yellowstone.

Graham felt like one of the family and that freaked him out just a little—but not too much. He liked the Trents and enjoyed hanging out with them.

The talk centered on the wedding. Everyone agreed it had been absolutely beautiful. Not to mention a really good time.

By two that afternoon, Graham had to go. There was plenty of work waiting for him back home at Callahan Canyon. He kissed Cassie goodbye outside on the front steps. Grinning, she waved as he drove away.

At home, he tracked down a couple of strays, fixed a busted fence and accomplished a bunch of other small chores he should have taken care of days ago. That night, he had a hard time staying home. He wanted to jump in his truck again, drive over to Cassie's place and see what she was up to, maybe convince her to come back to his house with him.

Somehow he controlled himself. He spent a couple of hours online managing his investments and turned in early. Monday, he put in a full day of work on the ranch. He'd left stew in the slow cooker that morning, so when dinnertime came, he invited his brothers over to eat.

Colter, Ash and Archer sat around his kitchen table eating his food—and razzing him. They wanted to know what the hell he'd been up to.

"We hardly see you these days," said Ash.

"Hey. There's a lot to do," Graham reminded his smirking brother. "I mean, what with the mayor's race and all."

"And Cassie Trent." Archer just had to put his two cents in. "There seems to be a lot to *do* between the two of you, too."

"Smart ass," Graham muttered under his breath.

Archer shrugged. "The past few weeks, you see more

of her than you do of your own brothers. That's just a plain fact."

Ash laughed. "Can't blame the man for that. Cassie Trent is mighty fine." He slanted Graham a knowing look. "But just watch yourself, big brother. Don't go gettin' your heart broke, you hear?"

Graham put on a confident smile. "Don't you worry. I know what I'm doing. Cassie and me, we understand each other."

"Way I heard it," Colter remarked cautiously, "she's very…independent. So you best not get your hopes up."

Graham didn't argue the point. Instead, he said, "We get along, the two of us. I like her a lot." *A whole lot* whispered an irritating voice in his head.

Archer said, "Rumor has it, she literally broke Jake McGeorge. He left town when he lost her."

"Listen," Graham answered coolly. "A rumor and five bucks will get you a coffee and a doughnut at the Silver Spur Café."

"Leave the man alone, you two." Colter was watching him way too closely. "As long as you're happy, Graham, more power to you."

And Graham *was* happy. He loved being with Cassie— maybe too much. Lately, he was having trouble staying away from her.

Maybe he needed to make more of an effort to spend his free time on his own. It was okay to get together once or twice a week, but not day after day. After all, their arrangement wouldn't last forever, and they couldn't afford to pretend that it might.

Tuesday, after she'd groomed the horses, mucked stalls and milked her goats, Cassie took a quick shower and grabbed her keys to head over to Graham's.

She stopped herself on the way out to her truck—because, come on. He hadn't called or dropped by yesterday.

And she'd been all too aware of his absence. The entire day she'd kept expecting to see his pickup come rolling down the two-track road that went by the main house.

He never appeared.

And why should he? Their fake relationship didn't require his constant presence at her side. He was right not to show up on her doorstep every day. Cassie put her keys in her pocket and instead of driving to Graham's, she helped her mom around the house.

By dinnertime, she was pretty fed up with herself. Because despite her determination to put a bit of much-needed space between her and Graham, she was still waiting for him to show up. Or call. Or drop her a text for crying out loud.

At dinner, out of the blue, her mom said, "Just call him, why don't you?" As though Cassie had been dragging around the house, waiting for a word from him.

She'd done no such thing. Uh-uh. Absolutely not. She'd been helpful and cheerful, and there was no reason whatsoever for her mom to act like she was sitting there wishing that Graham Callahan would call.

Cassie smiled sweetly at Olive. "I have no idea what you're talking about, Mom."

"Of course you don't," said her mother gently. "Never mind."

Cassie kept her mouth shut after that. It seemed the wiser course.

Graham did call two hours later as she was on her way to the goat pen for the evening milking. She stared at the lit up screen and ached to answer that call.

But she didn't. She sent it to voicemail and stuck the phone in her pocket. Later for him. She had evening chores to do.

The minute she returned to the house, she went straight up to her room and played back his message.

"Hey," his recorded voice said. "Just checking in. I've tried really hard to give you a little space." A self-conscious laugh escaped him. "Believe me. It wasn't easy…"

Did her heart melt into a puddle of goo at that point? No comment.

There was more to the message. "Anyway. I wanted to touch base about tomorrow. The debate's at seven. Hope you can make it. If you're going, let me pick you up? Give me a call."

She couldn't autodial him fast enough.

"Hi." His voice was low and just possibly a bit hesitant. She knew the feeling. "How're you doing?"

"Fine, Graham." She drew an oddly shaky breath and wondered what the heck was wrong with her. "And of course I'll attend the debate. That was our plan, after all."

"Good. How about if I pick you up?"

"I would like that."

"Excellent. And let's get an early dinner. Castillo's, if that works for you."

"Castillo's sounds really good." Already the cozy Mexican restaurant was starting to feel like *their* place, hers and Graham's. She frowned at the thought. Because how could she and Graham have a *place*? They were fake, and any *place* of theirs was merely part of the act.

Why did that make her feel so sad?

"I'll pick you up at four," he said.

"Four works."

A moment later, he said goodbye. She stood there with the phone in her hand, wondering why she felt so shaky and let down.

Graham tossed his phone on the nightstand and dropped to the edge of his bed. With a questioning whine, Izzy trotted over, plunked her head in his lap and wagged her bushy tail. As he scratched her behind the ears, he thought about Cassie. She'd seemed distant on the phone.

Was it him? Was it her?

Probably him—scratch that. It *was* him and he knew it, too. He'd created space between them, yesterday and then today. It had seemed like a good idea after her sister's beautiful, romantic wedding and the hours he and Cassie had spent together afterward.

Really, getting distance had been necessary. They needed to keep things in perspective, to remember that he was not Miles and she was not Renee.

They couldn't go getting carried away with the out-of-this-world chemistry they shared. He couldn't allow himself to become all wrapped up in how much he loved just being with her.

It wasn't going to go anywhere, he reminded himself for the hundredth time. They knew that and they were both fine with it. In the long run, they each had their reasons not to make their fake relationship real.

But damn. The last two days without her had been brutal. He just wasn't ready to give her up yet.

And he could not wait to see her tomorrow...

Cassie and Graham walked into Castillo's at four-thirty the next afternoon. The restaurant was packed. Apparently, dinner before the debate had seemed like a good idea to a lot of folks in town.

Cassie waved and mouthed greetings to the people she knew—which was just about everyone. They waited half an hour for a table. Cassie thought it was time well spent. People had questions for Graham about his stance on this or that issue, and he said where he stood and then explained his position.

Marty Moore was there. He gave Graham a hand flick of a wave and Cassie a sour little smile.

"Such a smooth operator, that Marty," Cassie whispered to Graham after Yolanda had seated them and zipped off to put in their order. "He always looks like he's up to no good."

"Yeah. Like he's planning to ban Christmas and lock up any citizen who dares to be kind to a stranger."

She laughed. "You say it like you're kidding, but I wouldn't put anything past him."

"We are on the same page about Marty. We are on the same page about a lot of things." His voice had gone velvety.

She looked in his eyes and thought all kinds of stuff she had no business thinking. That he was like no other guy she'd ever known. That they had so much in common, a certain view of life that matched up just right. That they laughed at the same things, that he understood her and she *got* him. That she would rather be with him than any other human being on the planet up to and including Vicky and Renee.

That when he kissed her she wanted to grab on tight and never, ever let him go.

Cassie's mouth went dry.

Oh, boy, was she in trouble.

Because this…what she was feeling right now?

It was not what she'd signed on for.

"Hey." He seemed worried suddenly. "You okay?"

"Uh, yeah. Good. Fine."

"For a minute there, you looked really upset."

"Just hungry, I guess."

His eyebrows were crunched together—in concern. Or possibly confusion. But then he smiled. "You're in luck. Here's our food."

Yolanda, bless her sweet soul, had chosen that moment to appear with their tamale platters. She set the plates down with a flourish and rushed off to find out why no one had brought them their Cokes.

They ate the delicious meal that Cassie was too preoccupied to properly appreciate. People stopped by the table to wish Graham a successful debate.

Cassie smiled and nodded and put in her two cents now and then, thinking in a weirdly disconnected way that their fake romance had definitely worked for Graham's campaign. People seemed completely accepting of the two of them as a real couple, a pair of heartbreakers who'd finally seen the light—in each other. Folks in town looked at Graham not only with fondness now, but also with respect. His star was on the rise.

Too bad she herself no longer knew what was real and what wasn't. It didn't seem to matter how many times she reminded herself to keep things in perspective. Her foolish heart had ideas of its own.

It wasn't far from Castillo's to the Tenacity Town Hall. In fact, Graham had parked in the town hall lot and they'd walked to the restaurant. At a little after six, they headed back along Central Avenue to the old brick building with the clock tower above the entrance. It was a cool old clock with black iron hands and Roman numerals to match. Too bad it hadn't shown the correct time for as long as Cassie could remember.

Inside, their boots echoed on the stone floor. The woman at the front desk waved them on into the main hall with the offices of the town clerk and the mayor and a couple of meeting rooms branching off to the sides. They went on to the wide hallway in back where the double doors to the auditorium stood wide-open.

The town clerk greeted them just inside the doors. She handed out cards and short pencils. "Just jot down your questions," she said. "I'll collect the cards before we begin."

Inside, rows of chairs had been set up facing the stage, where a long table and a podium waited.

Cassie hung back.

Graham suggested, "How about I sit with you until things get started?"

"No way. This is your show. Get up there. I'll be right here." She patted his arm and then took a chair on the aisle in the back row.

He bent close. "Hey."

"Hmm?" Clutching her question card and stub of pencil, she looked up at him. Longing made her throat tight. How had this happened to her? She was supposed to be immune to feelings like this...

There was worry in his dark eyes. "You okay?"

"Of course." She blasted him with her most confident grin. "Go. Knock their socks off." He didn't move, so she added, "No worries. I'll be right here cheering you on."

"Okay, then." Still looking doubtful, he straightened and headed for the stage. People greeted him. He stopped to speak with most of them as more folks came in and took seats.

Ellis Corey, a local rancher and also a candidate, walked confidently past where she sat. He was a tall, goodlooking guy with ebony skin. Graham turned to him. The two shook hands and went up the stage steps together.

The auditorium was really filling up now. Cassie spotted her mom and dad. They appeared at the other end of her row and continued on toward the front without spotting her. She'd known they would be here. Her mom had said they were coming, and Ryder had agreed to handle the evening milking.

As she watched, her mom leaned toward her dad and whispered something in his ear. Cassie knew she should try to get their attention, maybe sit with them. But there was chaos in her mind and heart right now. Dealing with her mom would be one challenge too many.

Instead, she watched from the corner of her eye as her dad caught her mom's hand and led her to a pair of empty seats up in front.

Another candidate for mayor, JenniLynn Garrett, appeared. Married with three young children, JenniLynn was slim and blonde with a friendly way about her. She smiled and nodded and exchanged hellos with people as she moved toward the front. Graham and Ellis Corey greeted her warmly when she joined them at the long table up there on the stage.

By then, Cassie had spotted several more people she knew, including Roslyn Ainsly and Larinda Peach. Mostly, though, she kept her eyes facing front and pretended to be lost in thought. Nobody stopped to chat with her, which was just the way she wanted it.

Yes, she was behaving oddly. Too bad. She had all these

feelings right now, and she wasn't the least equipped to handle them effectively.

Because falling in love with her fake boyfriend?

In no way had that been part of the plan. She was Cassie Trent, after all. And Cassie Trent was done with love.

"Cards, please?" The town clerk stood in the aisle gazing down at her with a patient smile.

Cassie winced and held up her empty card. "Sorry. I got nothin'."

"It's all right, dear. You hang on to that. If you think of a question, we'll try to get to it. Just pass me the others."

"What others?" she asked, her mind stuck back there on the realization that she was long gone in love with her pretend boyfriend.

"Here you go." The woman in the chair next to her held out a stack of cards.

"Oh!" Cassie said, knowing she looked every bit as out of it as she felt. "Right…" She took the cards and gave them to the clerk, who finally moved on.

Time crawled. Cassie sat there gritting her teeth, waiting it out.

Marty Moore appeared at last. His shoulders back, his big belly leading the way, he marched to the front of the room, scattering *Howdys* and *Good-to-see-you's* as he went. Once he'd mounted the stage, he nodded dismissively at the three other candidates and took the remaining seat at the table.

Colin Purdy, a college student whose family owned a small ranch just outside the town limits, mounted the steps and moved behind the podium.

"Hello everyone!" Colin announced. "It's great to see so many of you here this evening…" He offered a couple of sentences about himself, explaining that he was a senior at the University of Montana, majoring in political science with a minor in communications. "I'm your host and moderator tonight."

Next, Colin laid out the format for the debate. The candidates would each get five minutes to introduce themselves. After that would come the questions submitted by the audience, which Colin would read from the cards the clerk had collected.

"I want to assure everyone," he said, "that each candidate will get equal time in each section, including at the end of the debate when the candidates will offer rebuttals and make closing statements."

As Colin wrapped up his introduction and the debate began, Cassie tried to put aside her own emotional upheaval. She did her best to focus on the candidates and what they had to say about themselves and their plans for Tenacity.

Graham did great, she thought. He was friendly, confident and well-spoken. Also, he had good ideas for how to put their struggling town back in the black. Both Ellis Corey and JenniLynn Garrett did well, too.

As for Marty, he was condescending and self-satisfied, as usual. Cassie tried not to scowl at everything he said. He directed derogatory remarks to each of his fellow candidates. When Colin called him on it, Marty ignored him and went right on behaving badly. Cassie was relieved when Marty finally wrapped it up.

Colin moved on to the audience questions. He made sure that each candidate had a chance to tackle a variety of issues. Aside from Marty and his mean-spirited digs at his fellow candidates, Cassie thought the event was going well. Graham, JenniLynn and Ellis all came across as sincere and thoughtful. She might have been a little bit prejudiced, but it seemed to her that Graham was a natural leader. He laid out his ideas simply and clearly.

But then came the rebuttal section in which each candidate had a chance to refute criticisms about their candidacy, their background or their plans for the town.

Marty went first. He threw out the guidelines and went after JenniLynn instead.

"Let's talk about you, Mrs. Garrett," he said. "I don't see how a full-time homemaker with three kids is going to have a prayer of running this town successfully. Being mayor is a *real* job. Mrs. Garrett, you obviously don't have the temperament, the time or the skill to take on the tough task of leading Tenacity anywhere but deeper into debt."

A murmur of protest went up from the crowd.

Colin piped up with, "Mr. Moore, will you please confine yourself to—"

"Excuse me, Colin," JenniLynn cut in. "But I'm more than happy to respond to that accusation. Marty, you are so wrong. I'm a woman who can put in a full day of work on the family ranch, care for three children, keep the family budget in the black and be ready to take on any other challenges that might come my way. I assure you I will bring the necessary skills and dedication to the job of mayor. I know how to prioritize and I get things done.

"And Marty, I would like to add that, right now, you're in no position to be pointing your finger at me. *You're* the mayor now and what have *you* done to get us out of the mess we're in?"

Marty's scowl deepened. "I've done a damn fine job and that's just a plain fact. As for you, Mrs. Garrett, I call them as I see them. And you aren't equipped to be mayor of this town."

Once more, Colin tried to cut in. "Please, Mr. Moore—"

"Quiet, kid. I'm talkin' here." He swung on JenniLynn again. "Do yourself and everyone else in this town a favor. Drop out of the race and concentrate on your home and your family."

"I always put my family first," replied JenniLynn. "But as for dropping out of the race, I will do no such thing."

"And I'm glad to hear that," said Ellis Corey. "We need good people stepping up to save our town."

Stay out of it, Corey," growled Marty. "What do *you* know? Nothin'. You've got no more business trying to convince these good people that you can be mayor than Mrs. Garrett here does."

"I grew up in this town," Ellis said proudly. "My family has deep roots here, and my commitment to making life better here for everyone is real."

Someone in the audience shouted, "You tell him, Ellis!"

Ellis Corey wasn't finished. "I've seen what goes on, and I'm in a lot better position to guide this town into the future than you are, Marty Moore."

"Please." Colin tried again. "Everyone, if we could just—"

"You're all hat and no cattle!" Marty blustered at Ellis. "As for Mrs. Garrett, here, I'll say it again. Mrs. Garrett has a job to do at home. Her children need her, and she's got no business fooling around in politics. That's a plain fact and she ought to know that."

"Oh, come on." Graham was shaking his head. "That's just sexist garbage, and everyone in this room knows it. Talk about yourself, Marty. The hard truth is, you're only acting mayor now because Clifford Woodson chose you as his deputy mayor. And I agree with JenniLynn. You've done little to nothing to turn things around since taking

Woodson's place. If anybody's not fit here, it's you, Marty, plain and simple."

"Uh-oh," said someone down the row from Cassie. People shifted in their seats and whispered furtively to each other. Cassie understood why, too. Marty Moore was belligerent and mean-spirited in the best of circumstances. Under pressure, the man had a reputation for being downright vicious.

Marty's walrus mustache twitched. "Talk about unfit!" He pounded a fist on the table. "We all know what you are, Graham Callahan. A dang poser, that's what. All style, no substance."

"Give it up, Marty," Graham replied. "You are living in a glass house, and you'd best stop throwing stones. From where I'm sitting, you're the one with the problem. You've done a poor job as interim mayor, and now you refuse to deal with people's questions about all the things you *haven't* done."

"And that is the truth!" shouted a guy in the middle of the third row. Roslyn and Larinda, who were sitting directly behind him, clapped and whistled.

"All right, everyone…" Colin patted the air with both hands. "Calm down, now. Let's get back on track, please."

"Sit down and shut up, kid!" Marty bellowed. "I'm not done talkin' here." He shifted his beady gaze back to Graham. "You're not only a poser, Callahan, you're a fake through and through. You broke one too many hearts in this town to have a prayer of earning the trust of these good people—so what'd you do when you decided to run for mayor? You went out and hired Cassie Trent to be your steady girlfriend in a transparent effort to make yourself into someone you're not."

For a moment, Cassie couldn't believe what she'd just

heard. And then there was a ringing in her ears. She knew her face was cherry red with—what?

Embarrassment? Outrage? Misery?

Or all of the above?

No, Graham hadn't hired her to date him. But Marty's made-up accusation was painfully close to the truth. How could he have known that she and Graham weren't quite what they seemed to be?

The debate raged on. Marty went low and when that didn't work, he went even lower.

Cassie hardly heard any of it. She was still trying to figure out how Marty had guessed that she and Graham weren't for real.

Thinking back, there *was* that first day she'd ever really talked to Graham—that day at the Silver Spur Café. Marty was there, lurking in the background, watching. Listening.

Graham had announced his candidacy that day. Of course Marty would have instantly started looking for ways to discredit Graham as an opponent.

And Marty *had* turned up a lot when she and Graham were together. Was he spying on them all along? It seemed that he must have been, that he'd been watching them and eventually he'd come up with a theory—one that was uncomfortably close to the truth.

Up on the stage, Graham laid into Marty. "You must be desperate for a win, Marty, the way you keep attacking your fellow candidates. This is low, this behavior, even for you. If you have an issue with me, bring it on. But you leave my girl out of it."

My girl...

It sounded so real when Graham said it.

But she knew that it wasn't. Graham liked her, even

cared for her. But it wasn't love and it never would be—not for him. He'd made that fact achingly clear.

Up on the stage, Marty spewed more lies. Graham, JenniLynn and Ellis took turns knocking down every ridiculous accusation. It was tense and it was fiercely combative.

Cassie couldn't take it, not now, not with all the turmoil raging inside her. She needed fresh air. She couldn't sit in that chair for one more minute. She had to get out of there.

Rising, she stepped into the aisle, spun on her heel and headed for the double doors. Dropping her empty question card and bit of pencil on the table there, Cassie fled out into the wide hallway and headed for the front of the building.

The arched doors to the street were wide-open. She kept going right through them and down the stone steps.

Outside, the shadows had lengthened. As she stood there on the sidewalk, trying to decide what to do next, the Trailways bus rolled into town headed toward Bronco. She watched it go by, heard the whoosh of the air brakes as the bus eased to a stop in front of that bench she and Graham had sat on the first night they met up at the Social Club.

Tears filled her eyes at the memory of that night, when everything was fun and easy. When pretending to be Graham's true love had seemed like a grand idea, one that would neatly solve both his problem and hers.

Cassie started walking, heading for the driveway that led to the parking lot behind the town hall. The lot was full now. She wished with all her heart that she'd brought her own pickup.

But no. As Graham's fake true love, she'd ridden to this disaster with him. She marched through the lot until she reached his crew cab. He'd left it unlocked, so she climbed in.

While she waited for the debate to break up and Graham to drive her home, she considered her situation. Her conclusion: This whole thing with Graham had gone too far, and she had no one to blame but herself. Leaning back against the headrest, she closed her eyes and willed herself to drop off to sleep.

No such luck.

She was wide-awake when the good citizens of Tenacity began pouring into the parking lot. At least the gathering darkness outside offered her privacy from prying eyes. She watched the people she'd known all her life climb into their trucks and leave.

The lot was half-empty when Graham pulled open the driver's side door. The cab light burst on.

"Cassie. There you are."

She met his eyes. He looked worn out. No doubt from being verbally assaulted by Marty Moore for the last hour or so. "You okay?" she asked.

He climbed in and shut the door. "Of course I am. The question is, what about you?"

Carla and Duke Kleinsasser, who owned a few acres and a weathered farm-style house a few miles from town, got into the battered pickup parked on her side of Graham's truck. Carla, behind the wheel, waved at Cassie. She waved back as Carla pulled out of the space.

Graham said, "Cassie?" in a worried tone.

She turned to him. "Hmm?"

"Are *you* okay?"

She started to lie and say she was fine. Then again, he wouldn't buy it anyway, so why even try? "I've been better. But I'll live."

"When you left, I almost jumped down off the stage and ran out after you."

She wanted to hug him for that. But she kept her grabby hands to herself. "You're sweet. It's best that you didn't, though. Your running after me would only give Marty an excuse to say more rotten things about you—and me, as well."

He draped an arm over the steering wheel and stared out the windshield at the side of the building. "I wish I could say you were wrong about that."

People were still leaving, opening and shutting car doors, gunning their engines and heading for home. She said, "Let's get out of here, okay?"

"Good idea." He started the crew cab and carefully backed out of the space.

She waited until they were halfway to Stargazer Ranch before asking reluctantly, "I take it that it didn't get any better after I left?"

He shot her a quick glance. "Let me put it this way. Not knocking Marty into next week was a real challenge for me. But somehow, I managed it. Instead of beating the interim mayor to a pulp, I said that you're the best thing that ever happened to me and there is nothing fake about what we have together."

In other words, he'd lied. "Thank you. For…defending me."

"I probably should've just punched the guy."

"No, you shouldn't. You handled it perfectly—and what happened next?"

"Marty ranted some more, but by then most of the folks in the audience were as ready to strangle him as I was. Your high school friends, Larinda and Roslyn, made lots of rude noises and shouted at him to shut up."

Cassie almost smiled at that. "They're bold, those two."

"Oh, yes they are. Anyway, Marty finally stopped

making a fool of himself, and Colin managed to get things back on track. The rest of the event went pretty smoothly."

"I'm glad to hear it. From what I saw before I left, you did good."

He slanted her a warm glance. "I appreciate that. And aside from Marty making a complete ass of himself, I do think it went well."

They drove the rest of the way to the ranch in silence.

When they got there, her mom's Yukon was parked in front of the house and the lights were on in her parents' room upstairs. Graham pulled to a stop behind her mom's car and turned off the engine.

He laid his lean arm across the back of her seat. They stared at each other, sharing a silence that was far from comfortable. She saw the worry in his eyes.

"What is it?" he asked. "Talk to me."

She folded her hands in her lap and looked down at them as she tried to figure out how to begin. "You handled Marty beautifully, you really did."

He tried a laugh. It fell flat. He seemed to be studying her face. "Cassie. What's going on?"

Her mouth was dry and her throat had clutched. But she swallowed hard and pushed out the words that truly did need saying. "Well, Graham, about you and me and our, um, dating arrangement. I can't help but think that it's gone too far."

"Too far?" He raked his unruly hair back from his forehead. "No. Come on, Cassie. You can't take what Marty says seriously. He'll try anything to mess with the competition. The man has no shame."

"Listen. Please…" *I care too much*, she was thinking. *I care too much and it hurts and this has to stop.* "I think it's time that we put a little distance between us."

His eyes narrowed. "No! Cassie, that's a bad idea. If we do that, we're just letting Marty win."

"I don't think so. We don't have to put out a press release about it. We can just let people go on thinking that we're a couple. But it's time that we stopped this, time we went our separate ways."

"Because of Marty, that's what you're saying, right?" he asked in a ragged voice. "What he said tonight really did get to you."

It seemed only right to answer him honestly. "Yeah, it did get to me. It made me feel like a liar and a cheat."

"But you're not—"

"Listen. Please. This thing with us, it was fun and exciting at first. I really thought nobody would get hurt..." Should she tell him the rest of it, reveal that the biggest problem was her hopeless heart? She *wanted* Graham. In the real way. The forever way. And she was so tempted to simply keep going as they had been, to keep on pretending that they were more than they would ever be for as long as he was willing to play that game.

But they weren't a real couple. And the longer they kept on with this, the harder it would be for her when the end finally came.

She'd thought she was immune to love. But no. She was just like everyone else. Love had found her at last.

Wouldn't you know it had happened with a man who'd made it crystal clear that he was done with love and wouldn't be changing his mind about that anytime soon?

Graham didn't want to give up.

He should tell her the truth—that he was gone on her, that he wanted to be her guy for real. He should ask her if maybe she might be willing to give him a real chance.

Because he *did* want to be her guy. He wanted to be her one and only. Her impossible, perfect forever...

He had this problem that lately he couldn't picture his life without her in it. But did that mean he was ready to deny the lesson he'd learned the hard way from his cheating runaway bride and his backstabbing best friend?

No.

Cassie was right. They were in too deep, and the wise move now was to turn and walk away.

"Graham." Her voice was hollow, hushed.

"Yeah?"

"You know I'm right."

He made himself look at her—it wasn't easy. She was so beautiful, and it hurt like hell to realize that he wouldn't be seeing her anymore.

Except maybe now and then, in passing.

And in his dreams.

"All right," he said, his voice flat, defeated. "I get it. I do." The silence fell between them again, pressing in.

But then she spoke. "I've had the best time with you." Her eyes were enormous. Was she crying? He hoped not. If she cried, well, that just might break him.

"It has been wonderful," he said gruffly.

"I wish you all the good things, Graham."

"I wish the same for you." He watched as she leaned on the passenger-side door. "Wait," he said. She frowned but took her hand off the door. "Let's do this right, okay?"

She drew a shaky breath. "Um, sure. Okay..."

He jumped out, ran around to her side, pulled her door open and offered his hand. For a fraction of a second, she hesitated. But then her fingers touched his. He grabbed on tight and wished he would never have to let go.

She stepped down and he settled her hand in the crook

of his arm. Together, they went through the low gate and up the walk. Too soon, they stood at the front door.

"Cassie…" He took her gently by her shoulders and turned her toward him. Cradling her beautiful face in his palms, he lowered his mouth to hers.

She sighed. He did, too. They didn't go deep, but that kiss was so tender, so sweet and slow.

When he raised his head, he watched her eyelids flutter open. "Goodbye, Cassie."

"Bye, Graham."

And then he made himself turn, walk back down the steps, get in his truck and drive away.

Chapter Eleven

Early the next morning after a mostly sleepless night, Cassie crawled from her bed, threw on some work clothes and went downstairs.

Her mom was waiting for her. "There you are!" Olive grabbed her in a hug and then took her by the shoulders. "We missed you last night at the debate."

"I was there. Just, you know, keeping a low profile."

Her mother's eyes shone with concern. "How *are* you?"

"I'm okay, Mom. Honestly."

"Well," said Olive. "I'm not. I'm outraged. That Marty Moore," she muttered. "We need to be rid of him and that big, ugly mouth of his, too. I swear to you, Cassie. That man will never get elected mayor of this town. I can't wait until Graham beats the pants off him. Then Marty can slink back to whatever rock he crawled out from under. Where does he get off? Who does he think he is? No one is voting for him and he's bound to find that out the hard way."

Cassie could not have agreed with her more. "I think Marty's going to be sharply reminded that he's never actually been elected mayor and when it comes time for the citizens of Tenacity to make their choice, no one is going to be voting for him."

"Yep." Olive pulled her close for a second hug, then held her away again and added, "You just wait. Come November, Graham will be elected mayor of our town."

She tried a smile. "No doubt about that," she said, and turned for the coffeepot.

While her mom continued ranting against Marty Moore and Clifford Woodson and all the political insiders who had come so close to destroying Tenacity, Cassie ate a bowlful of homemade goat milk yogurt and filled her travel mug with coffee. "Gotta go, Mom. Chores need doing."

Olive grabbed her in yet another hug. "You are not to let what Marty Moore said bother you for one single second," she whispered hotly into Cassie's ear.

"I won't," Cassie promised—and made her escape.

For the next several hours, she gathered eggs, milked her goats and mucked out the barn. Finally, around eleven, she ran upstairs for a quick shower.

At a quarter of twelve, in clean jeans and a fresh T-shirt, she headed for Vicky's apartment above the grocery story. Because there were times in a woman's life when she needed her lifelong friend more than she needed to draw her next breath.

Vicky took one look at her and pulled her inside. "What *happened*?"

"I ended it with Graham."

Vicky said a bad word. Then she pulled Cassie close and hugged her hard. "Mint Chocolate Chip?"

Cassie moaned. "Yes. Please."

So Vicky dished them up giant helpings of ice cream, and they sat down at the table to shovel it in.

"You missed the debate," Cassie said.

"Yeah. I just couldn't bring myself to go."

"I don't blame you." Cassie filled her in on all of it—from the ugly things Marty Moore had said to what had happened when Graham took her home.

"That Marty Moore," Vicky said when she was done. "What a weasel. And as for you and Graham, well, it's for the best and you know it."

Cassie ate another giant spoonful of ice cream. "I do know. Calling it off with him was the right thing to do."

"I mean, *you* don't want a relationship and neither does he."

"Exactly." So then why did it hurt so much to think of her life stretching out before her without Graham in it? She didn't get it. She *loved* her life.

Or she had. Until now.

"Cass, you know how men are…"

"Whoa, now, Vick. Hold on a minute. This is not about how *bad* men are."

"Okay, but I'm just saying—"

"Please, Vick. I love you so much. But I think you're wrong. In fact, Graham is amazing. And as for Butch and Craig and Jake, they're good guys. My dad and my brothers are, as well. I mean, Ryder makes me want to punch him out now and then, but overall—"

"Fine. There are some good ones." Vicky wrinkled her nose as though she smelled something bad. "But as a rule, anyone with a Y chromosome is not to be trusted."

"That's just not true. And to be crystal clear, it's not Graham's fault that I'm miserable right now. He's been honest with me from the first. He doesn't want a real relationship—and neither do I."

Aw, Cass…" Vicky's voice had softened. She dropped her spoon into her bowl, reached across the little table and squeezed Cassie's arm. "I hesitate to say it, especially after making all that noise about how much I hate men, but you just don't sound all that convincing."

"About what?"

"About how you don't want a real relationship."

"But I *don't*!"

Vicky looked at her so patiently now. "Get honest. You like Graham. You *really* like him. Enough that suddenly you're having trouble trying to tell me how you're through with love."

"But I *am* through with love."

"Give it up." Vicky wore the sweetest, saddest little smile. "You care for Graham Callahan. A lot. You know that you do."

"It doesn't matter. Graham and I are through. It was fake in the first place and now it's over."

Vicky's chair scraped the floor as she stood. She took Cassie by the arm and pulled her up, too.

"Let go," Cassie protested glumly.

"Uh-uh. Come on." Vicky pulled her in close for another hug. "It will be all right," she whispered as she patted Cassie's back.

"Oh, I don't think so…"

Vicky pulled away then. "Fine then. Have it your way. It *won't* be okay, not as long as you mope around, denying your real feelings and telling yourself it's hopeless."

"Because it *is* hopeless. The man has been completely messed over by the woman he truly loved. He said he's not ever trying again and I believe him."

With a groan, Vicky dropped back into her chair. "This can't be happening."

Cassie looked down at her. "What can't be happening?"

Vicky was shaking her head. "I cannot possibly be thinking that you should try again with this guy, that you should go to him and tell him you love him and give him a chance to say it back to you. Uh-uh. No way. I'm not the friend who does that."

"Are you saying you think I should tell Graham the truth about how I feel?"

"I'm not saying what you should do, Cass. It's not my call. But you know I love you, right?" At Cassie's nod, she added, "And however it all ends up, just know that I'm here and I'm on your side and one way or another, you're going to be fine."

"Oh, Vick. I hope so…"

When Cassie got home an hour later, she discovered that Adelaide had once again escaped the goat pen. Plus, a couple of the more adventurous does had squeezed through the fence break, too. The three miscreants were happily munching clover right there in the big meadow between the pen and the ranch road. Cassie repaired the fence and put them back inside it. Then she helped her mom with dinner and volunteered to handle the cleanup herself.

She went to bed early. Fat lot of good that did. She spent the night waiting for sleep to settle over her. It never happened.

"You look like death warmed over," her mother declared disapprovingly when Cassie came downstairs in the morning.

"Love you, too, Mom," she muttered, and headed for the coffeepot.

"What's wrong?" Olive demanded.

She filled her travel mug. "Nothing, Mom." Turning, she leaned against the counter and sipped. "Nothing at all."

"You know I don't believe you. Whatever it is, when you're ready to talk about it, I'm here to listen."

She almost took her mom up on that offer. But Olive Trent was a woman of action. If Cassie confessed that she'd ended it with Graham and really wished she hadn't, Olive might do just about anything—up to and including tracking the man down, explaining that Cassie was miserable without him and begging the guy to give her daughter one more chance.

No.

Her mom meant well. But Cassie didn't need any help with the Graham situation right now. Because there was no Graham situation. It was over. Finished. Done.

She put the lid on her travel mug and headed out to work.

The day dragged by. She was absolutely miserable. She'd broken up with Graham on Wednesday night and it was only Friday. The past two days had felt like a lifetime of loneliness and misery. How long would this feeling of sad hopelessness go on?

She decided not to think about that. It would get better, she reminded herself over and over. All she had to do was keep her chin up and get through each day.

She'd thought she loved Butch and Craig and Jake, hadn't she? And her love hadn't lasted. Her love could not be trusted. She was a bad bet in the forever department.

Plus, Graham didn't want her anyway—not in the lifetime kind of way.

It couldn't work. They both knew it. It was better that she'd ended it now.

Renee and Miles and their two dogs got home from Yellowstone at five. They joined Cassie, Ryder and the parents for dinner that evening. Renee seemed to glow with happiness, and Miles, always a serious, self-contained sort of man, looked like he'd found the secret of life.

He probably had. It was obvious that he and Renee were a match for the ages.

After dinner, Miles kissed his wife and headed back to their bungalow with Jasper trotting happily along beside him. Renee stuck around to help with the dishes. Her dad wandered off to watch some old Clint Eastwood western in the living room, and Ryder left to meet up with some friends. Cassie, Renee and their mom cleaned up the kitchen together.

When that job was done, Olive kissed Cassie on the cheek, gave Renee a hug and went into the other room to join their dad.

Renee hung up the dish towel. "Come on. It's nice out, and you have some time before you need to deal with the goats. Let's catch up."

They sat on the front step with Buddy sprawled on the porch close to Renee. The day was slowly fading. Cassie looked up at the wisps of cloud in the sky—and thought of Graham.

Because everything lately made her think of Graham.

It was a serious problem. She couldn't sleep at night. And she was tired and lonely all day.

Lonely for the guy she'd sent away...

Renee scooted closer. "It's Graham, isn't it?"

Cassie stifled a groan. "What did Mom say to you?"

Renee smiled tenderly. "Mom said nothing to me about Graham. Not one word. She does look kind of worried, though."

"I'm not ready to get into it with her yet."

"Get into...?"

"What I mean is, I want your advice, I really do. But will you please keep whatever I say tonight to yourself?"

Renee nodded. "I will, I promise."

Cassie shrugged in resignation. "Wednesday night, I ended it with Graham."

"Oh, no…"

"Yeah. It's over."

"But what *happened*?"

"Nothing. Everything…"

"Well, that clears it all up," Renee replied dryly. Then she frowned. "Wait. Wednesday was the mayoral debate, right?"

"Right." Cassie filled Renee in on all that had gone down that night.

When she fell silent, her sister said, "So… Marty Moore was his usual insufferable self. Things got ugly, but Graham and the other candidates stood up to him and shut him down."

"More or less, yeah."

"And then you broke up with Graham."

"Yeah."

"But Cassie, why did you break up with Graham—and by that I mean, what's really going on?"

"Renee, you have no idea…"

"So enlighten me. Please."

"Trust me. You don't want to hear it."

"I'll be the judge of that. Talk."

Stalling some more, Cassie stared off toward the mountains. Renee simply waited her out. Finally, she gave in and admitted, "Well, Graham and I, we made a deal…"

Renee sat there, not interrupting even once as Cassie laid it all out. She explained that she'd needed a guy to get Olive off her back and that Graham had thought a fake girlfriend would ease people's fears that he was not settled and serious enough to be mayor. "We came to an agreement. It seemed to work for both of us. Mom adores Graham, and people in town loved seeing us together. It was all great fun, too. I mean, Graham and I really do like each other…"

Her sister draped a comforting arm across her shoulders. "But…"

"But nothing. It was good for both of us. Nobody was supposed to get hurt."

"And yet you suddenly broke up with him."

"Yeah, well. I didn't know what to do. I was starting to get too attached."

"And that's bad?"

"Of course, it's bad."

"Why?"

"You know me. When it comes to love and all that, my track record sucks."

"You mean because of what happened with Butch and Craig and Jake."

"That's right. They were great guys, and I broke up with all three of them. Poor Jake left town because of me."

"Cassie. Did Jake tell you it was all your fault that he was leaving?"

"Well, no. But the whole town seems to think that he left because I broke his heart."

"That doesn't make it true."

"Fair enough. But he was really upset with me when I called it off with him."

"Okay, but the fact is, you don't really know what reason or reasons made him pick up stakes and move along—plus, even if he'd told you his leaving was all about you, it was still his choice. It's not like you ran the guy out of town."

"People said—"

"Stop." Renee threw up both hands. "Who cares what people said? That's called gossip and it's not the least bit dependable. Jake wasn't the right guy for you. Neither was Craig or Butch. That doesn't necessarily mean that Graham isn't, either. I saw the two of you together—saw the way you two laugh at the same things, the way you guys seem to have whole conversations without saying a word. You and Graham are close, like best friends."

Cassie's throat felt tight. She swallowed hard. Suddenly, she was blinking away tears. "You're right. It's like when I broke up with Graham, I broke up with my best friend. Like I just woke up one day and decided I was cutting Vicky from my life…"

Renee pulled a tissue from her pocket and handed it over.

"Thanks." Cassie sniffled and dabbed at her eyes. "Sheesh. I'm a mess."

"Nah. You're just like everyone else. Falling in love is beautiful, yeah. But it's scary, too. It's like…walking off a cliff and trusting the one you love to catch you when you fall. You could get badly hurt. It's nothing to be taken lightly."

Cassie laid her head on her sister's shoulder. "I don't know what to do."

Renee gently stroked her hair. "Well, for what it's worth, I think Graham is in love with you, too."

Cassie's silly heart leapt at those words. She ordered it to calm the heck down and said flatly, "*I* don't."

Renee didn't argue. Instead, she advised, "You should

go to him, talk to him honestly. Maybe he thinks he's doing the noble thing by staying away."

Cassie laughed through her tears. "Graham. Noble. He would never admit to that. He'd make a joke about it."

"Like I said, the two of you have a whole lot in common."

Graham spent Saturday morning in the east pasture with Colter and Ash and a couple of chain saws. Together, they removed a giant cottonwood that had been split by a lightning strike back in May.

Half the tree was already on the ground. Once they'd felled the other half, they cut the wood into manageable lengths, loaded it into the bed of one of the ranch trucks and took it back home for firewood. After stacking the fresh-cut logs on a pair of racks, they covered the green wood with tarps to keep the rain and snow off it. They would leave it to season for a full year before it would be dry enough to burn.

Colter said, "I've got a pot roast in the slow cooker at my place. Takers?"

"Me!" Ash raised a hand.

Graham had appreciated the distraction of dealing with the damaged tree, but lunch with his brothers included too much good-natured ribbing and joking around. Lately—to be specific, since Wednesday night when he and Cassie called it off—he was in no mood for joking around. "Thanks, but I've got leftovers at my place."

Ash and Colter shared a look but refrained from comment, which Graham appreciated. Yeah, he'd been feeling low, and he knew that he needed to make an effort to snap out of it.

But not today.

With Izzy at his heels, he went home, heated up a slab of last night's meat loaf and ate it standing up, staring blindly out the window over the sink.

He was shoving another forkful into his mouth when a late model Subaru pulled into the driveway. "What the...?" He blinked in disbelief as Victoria Woodson, of all people, got out and came up the stone walk.

He was still standing at the window, clutching the plate with his half-eaten meat loaf on it when she knocked. For a minute or two, he stood in frozen disbelief that she was at his front door. Then she knocked a second time. He blinked, shook himself and went to answer.

Izzy beat him to it. She was already in the entry area wagging her tail at the door when he got there.

"Go lie down," he commanded. With a whimper of protest, Izzy turned and headed for the living area.

Graham pulled the door wide. "Victoria. Hey."

"Hello, Graham." Folding her arms across her chest, she looked him up and down. "Listen. Can we talk?"

"Uh, yeah. Sure." He stepped back. "Come on in." He led her past the doorway to the kitchen and into the main living area. "Have a seat."

She perched on the leather chair by the French doors that led out to the deck. Graham took the easy chair next to the fireplace. Izzy, who'd been waiting on the fireplace rug, made a beeline for their guest.

"If she bothers you—"

"She's fine." Victoria cut him off and gave the dog a pat on the head. Izzy immediately flopped down at her feet. Victoria stared at the dog for a long count of five. When she looked up again, she asked, "Did I interrupt your lunch?"

He realized she could see his half-eaten plate of meat

loaf sitting where he'd left it on the counter that separated the kitchen from the living area. "No. I mean, I wasn't that hungry anyway." But was *she*? "Want some meat loaf?"

Did she almost smile? It kind of seemed like it, and that surprised him. Victoria Woodson came across as super-serious—or maybe he only thought that because he'd always had the feeling that he was not her favorite person.

"No, thanks," she said. "I'm good."

"All right then…" He had no idea what to say next. Was this about Cassie somehow? His heart was galloping madly and had been since Victoria pulled into his driveway.

Because it *had* to be about Cassie, didn't it? He couldn't think of any other reason Cassie's best friend might be sitting in his living room right now.

Victoria cleared her throat. "Well, I'll just get right down to it, if that's okay with you?"

"Yeah. Good. Just…whatever it is, lay it on me."

"First, I need something from you."

"Sure. What?"

Victoria's momentary smile had vanished. Now she was scowling at him. "I need the truth and nothing but the truth. Can you give me that?"

"Uh. Yeah. The truth. You got it—about what?"

"Are you or are you not in love with Cassie?"

He shocked the hell out of himself when he didn't even hesitate, just opened his mouth and said, "Yeah. I *am* in love with Cassie. Very much so."

Vicky gave a severe little nod. "All right, then. Cassie loves you, too. She's just afraid to admit it."

Something bloomed in the center of his chest right then. It just might have been hope. He asked cautiously, "You sure about that?"

"I am, yes. But because of her, er, previous relationships, she doesn't trust her own heart. She blames herself for how things turned out for her in the past."

"I know that. She told me all about those other guys— that she broke their hearts and she feels guilty about it and she's decided she's just not going there again."

Vicky let out a groan. "She told you everything."

"Yeah…"

"You do know what that means, don't you?"

"Uh. Not really. What?"

"Graham, Cassie not only loves you, but she also *trusts* you."

He gulped. "You just said it again."

"It?"

"You said that she loves me."

"So?"

"Do you really mean that, Victoria? Cassie loves *me*?"

"Oh, yeah." Victoria scowled. "She's a goner. There's no going back. I don't get it. I don't get how any woman can hand over her trust and love to a man. But that's just me, and right now, this isn't about me. It's about my best friend's heart, which now belongs to you—whether she's willing to tell you how she feels about you or not."

Graham was pretty much speechless at that point.

Not that Victoria cared. She swept to her feet and announced, "So I think you should go to her, tell her you love her and take it from there."

He just stared.

"Well?" Victoria demanded.

"Um. Yeah! I will do that, right away."

"Good."

"And thank you, Victoria. I mean that. Thank you so much."

She narrowed her dark eyes at him. "Don't screw it up."

"I won't," he vowed. "I swear to you I won't."

She headed for the door with Izzy right behind her, as Graham jumped up from his chair to see her out. He'd taken two steps when Victoria whirled on him and put out a hand. "Stay there," she instructed. He and his dog froze simultaneously. "I can let myself out."

Izzy gave a whine of sheer disappointment as Cassie's friend disappeared into the narrow front hallway. A moment later, Graham heard the door open and shut. Not long after that, the Subaru started up and drove away.

For several more wasted seconds, he stood in the middle of his living room, hardly daring to believe what Cassie's friend had just said to him. Cassie trusted him. She *loved* him…

He lurched to life. Izzy fell in step behind him. He turned to tell her to stay.

But when he looked down at her eager face and wagging tail, he couldn't do it. "All right." He grabbed his keys and plunked his hat on his head. "Come on, then."

This time, Izzy's whine was a gleeful one.

With his dog at his heels, Graham made for the door.

A moment later, with Izzy panting happily in the passenger seat, he started his engine, put the pickup in gear and threw up a trail of dust all the way to paved road.

At Stargazer Ranch, he slammed to a stop in front of the main house and jumped from the crew cab. Not to be left behind, Izzy hopped over the console and gave him a please-let-me-come-with-you whimper from the driver's seat.

"Fine. Let's go."

She followed him through the gate and up the front steps.

"Sit," he said when they reached the door. Izzy sat right down. He was about to ring the bell when the door opened.

"Graham!" Olive cried gleefully. Then she scowled. "Where have you been?"

He swept off his hat—and evaded her question. "Well, Olive, you know how it goes sometimes. Ranch life can be real demanding."

"Translation: You're not going to tell me what's going on."

"Well, I was hoping to—"

"Never mind." Olive waved a hand. "You're as bad as Cassie. But at least you're here now." She gave his dog a melting smile. "And who's this adorable sweetheart?"

"This is Izzy."

"Ah. Well, come in, come in—both of you!"

He hesitated. "I was hoping… I mean, is Cassie here?"

Olive sighed dramatically. "It's the usual, I'm afraid. That troublemaking goat Adelaide got out *again*, and a few of the others squeezed out after her. Cassie has to catch them, pen them back up and repair the fence. Come on in and have a cool drink while you wait for her." Stepping back, she gestured him over the threshold.

"Thank you, Olive. But I think I'll go help Cassie with the goats."

Cassie's mom put her hand over heart. "Well, aren't you the gentleman? She will appreciate that." With a nod, he turned to go. "Oh, and Graham…" Tamping down his impatience to see Cassie, he faced Olive again and put on an attentive expression. Olive said sharply, "I just wanted you to know that it's going to be a great relief to most of us in this town when you win the mayor's race and kick Marty Moore out on his butt."

If he hadn't been so anxious to get to Cassie, he just

might have grabbed Olive in a hug. "I appreciate your belief in me, Olive. I honestly do."

"Of course, I believe in you. Do not let the crooks get you down."

"I won't," he promised.

"And work things out with my baby girl."

He almost smiled. "That's what I'm here for."

"Good, then. Get after it."

That time, when he and Izzy turned for the steps, Olive let them go.

Cassie had returned Adelaide and her fellow escapees to the pen and then blocked off the area of fence that needed repair.

The goats stood at the temporary barrier she'd erected and razzed her as she worked. "Maa…! Maa…!"

In the past, she would have laughed at them. They were cute in their complete lack of remorse for their latest breakout.

But today, she just felt glum and sad and didn't even have the energy to enjoy their feisty, can-do spirit. Instead, she worked doggedly, rolling out more mesh goat fencing and securing it to the posts. She was so busy trying to get the job done, she not only ignored the racket of the goats, but she hardly glanced up for long stretches of time.

Maybe, she was thinking, she'd made a bad choice here. Maybe she would have to quit moping around and do something about her broken heart.

She really needed to talk to Graham, to see if maybe—

Right then, she heard a dog whine. When she turned toward the sound, a familiar black-and-white border collie was staring up at her hopefully. "Izzy?"

The dog whined again and wagged her furry tail.

It couldn't be…

But then she looked out across the wide meadow and saw Graham striding toward her through the ankle-deep grass.

"Graham!"

He looked—so good. He looked like everything she'd learned the past few days that she could not live without. And then he took off his hat and he put it to his heart.

And he just kept on coming.

"Maa…! Maa…!" The goats cried.

And then she was running to meet him halfway with Izzy at her heels. "Graham!"

"Cassie!"

By then, he was running, too, both of them laughing like a pair of love-crazed fools. It only took a minute that lasted forever and then they collided. Dropping his hat to the grass he pulled her close.

"Cassie…" he whispered.

And she said, "Graham…"

A second later, his mouth was on hers, and everything flew away except the warmth and strength of his arms around her, the beating of his heart against her breasts— and that kiss. *His* kiss, the kiss she'd been longing for, the kiss she'd been so sure she would never share again.

"Maa…!" called the goats. Izzy, at their feet, let out a quick, happy bark.

Graham went on kissing her. She held on tight and kissed him right back for the longest, sweetest time.

Too soon, he was lifting his head.

Dazed with sheer happiness, she blinked up at him. "I missed you," she whispered. "And I…" She realized she had a thousand questions. "Are you okay? Has something happened? I'm so glad you're here and I… Well, I mean, what's going on?"

"Cassie, I…"

She was so thrilled to see him, she could hardly draw breath. "What, Graham? Whatever it is, it's okay, I promise you. Just tell me. Just…say it."

"I well, I…" He seemed to run out of words and that made her smile. As a rule, Graham Callahan never ran out of words. Gazing up at him, her heart beating so hard the sound echoed in her ears, she waited for him to say whatever he had on his mind. Finally, he said, "I, uh, realized something…" His face was flushed, his dark eyes gleaming. He really did look so very glad to see her.

She felt a lightness in her chest. It might have been joy, lifting her up, giving her hope that things might work out for them, after all. "What?" she demanded. "Tell me. Tell me now."

"It's just that I… Well, Cassie, I was wrong."

"Wrong about…?"

"Everything. All of it. Wrong to say I would never love again. Wrong to give up just because I got hurt bad once. Wrong not to stand tall and try again. Wrong not to somehow have known that the day would come when I would walk into the Silver Spur and there you would be, grinning at me, ready to give me a hard time and keep me on my toes—I mean, how could I not have known that the perfect woman for me was right here in my hometown all the time?" He pressed his rough palm to her cheek and whispered desperately, "Damn. It's been sheer hell since we broke it off." A single tear slid down her cheek. He wiped it away with a gentle stroke of his thumb. "Sweetheart. Don't cry…"

She sniffled—just a little. "Let me tell you, Graham

Callahan. I know exactly what you're talking about. It's been three days, the worst three days of my life. I missed you so much and I mean that sincerely."

"I hear you. It's been the same for me. Just, please, tell me that I have a chance with you, after all…"

She caught his face between her hands and cried, "A *chance*? Are you kidding? You'll never get rid of me now."

"Good." His voice was gruff and low. "Because I never want to let you go."

With shaking fingers, she brushed the shaggy dark hair at his temple as she whispered anxiously, "You sure?"

His expression was perfectly serious now, his gaze steady on hers. "I know I said that Serena and my so-called best friend messed me over so bad I would never love again. But then I walked into the Silver Spur a month ago and there you were. Since then, I've had to learn how wrong I've been. That was hard for me. I was pretty locked in to never trying again. But Cassie, I get it now. Serena was never the woman for me. You are. I love you. I do."

"Oh, Graham…" How to tell him? How to make him see? She just went ahead and said the words. "I hear you. And I love you, too."

For a moment, he seemed struck speechless. But then he said, low and rough, "Thank God for that. Thank God for *you*. Cassie, I…"

"What?" She put her hands on his broad shoulders and looked him square in the eye. "Just say it. Whatever it is, I can take it. It can't be that bad…"

"It's not bad, honestly, sweetheart. It's just that I saw how hard the debate was on you. I've stewed over that night a lot. And I've realized that no elected office is more important than you, not to me. I don't want us to be fake anymore, not in any way. And I don't ever want to see you put in a bad position because of me. Both Ellis Corey and JenniLynn Garrett have my full confidence. Either one of them would make a great mayor, and I think both will beat Marty Moore in November. So I'm going to withdraw from the race."

"What?!" She caught his face between her hands again. "What did you just say to me?"

"You heard me. I'm dropping out."

"Graham, no!"

He seemed puzzled. "No…?"

"I don't want you to drop out. I think you have a whole lot to offer our town—so no, uh-uh. You are not dropping out."

He was frowning. "You sure?"

"For my part, absolutely." Then she sighed. "But I get it. It *is* your choice."

He offered gently, "How about this? I will consider staying in the race."

"Good."

They stared at each other. She felt she saw their future in his eyes—a bright future filled with love and laughter, with everything that makes life worthwhile.

"Cassie…" He pulled her close again. Their lips met in a long, hungry kiss. When he lifted his head, he teased, "So then, if I win, you wouldn't have a problem with being the mayor's wife?"

She put on a stern expression. "Graham Callahan, is this an actual proposal?"

He didn't even blink. "You bet it is. Take your time thinking it over. Because I'm not going anywhere. I'll be waiting and hoping until you decide how it will be."

In the pen, the goats were still carrying on, sticking

their noses through the fence, bleating, "Maa... Maa... Maa!" Not far away, Izzy sat panting happily, her tail sweeping back and forth through the grass.

"Oh, Graham..."

"Yeah?" He looked at her so tenderly. "Tell me. What?"

She rested her hand against his heart. "This is like some dream—like all my wishes coming true. Until a few minutes ago, I was afraid I'd lost you forever—and now you are right here in front of me, asking me to marry you."

"Some say I'm a bit extra," he offered with a grin.

She laughed then. "You are, and I like it. I like it a lot."

He touched her cheek, his fingertips warm against her skin. "As for my proposal, I meant what I said. Take your time. Think it over."

"As if I'll be thinking about anything else."

"Just remember what Mike Cooper said that first night I took you to the Tenacity Social Club..."

She did remember. "Mike said, 'When it's right, it's right.' And I really think he might be onto something there."

"No doubt about that. And when it comes to you and me, Cassie, I'm as serious as a man ever gets. The truth is, my heart has belonged to you since that first day at the Silver Spur. You are like no woman I've ever known. You're not only beautiful. You're all heart and you are so strong. You can take care of yourself. I know you don't need me—or any man. But if you will have me, I'll spend my life making sure you'll never be sorry you chose to be mine."

Cassie thought of her past right then—and saw her own actions in a whole new light. She would always regret that she'd hurt three good men. But at least she'd made the right choice in saying no to them. It would never have lasted with any one of them. Because they weren't Graham. All this time, she'd only been waiting for the right man to finally come along.

"I love you, Graham Callahan," she said. "I honestly thought I wasn't cut out for love. But you proved me wrong. So yes, I will marry you."

"You're serious?" His voice was hushed, almost reverent.

"You bet I am."

"Damn. Cassie…" And he lifted her up and spun her around as he kissed her.

A few minutes later, they got to work repairing the fence.

Once that job was done, they went straight to the main house to break the big news to Olive.

Of course, Cassie's mom knew right away what was going on. Olive burst into tears at the sight of them holding hands in the front hall, with Izzy sitting happily at their feet. "Oh, my Lord!" she exclaimed on a sob. "You two do look happy!"

"We are!" Cassie grabbed her mom in a hug as the tears started flowing. "Mom! Hey! It's okay, it's good! We *are* happy, I promise you."

Her mom held her tight and sobbed against her shoulder. "Of course you are," Olive sniffled. "I can see it. I just *know*…"

"Oh, Mom. You know what, exactly?"

"That everything is working out the way I've dreamed it might." Olive pulled back enough to reach out a hand for Graham. He took it. "I can see the truth in your eyes," she said to him. "You love my daughter." It wasn't a question.

He nodded. "I do, Olive. With all my heart. I want to spend the rest of my life with Cassie."

"Glory be!" Olive grabbed Graham in hug. Sniffling some more, she said sternly, "You'd better take good care of my little girl."

"Olive, I will. I swear that I will."

A few minutes later, they heard the back door shut. By then, the three of them were sharing coffee at the kitchen table with Izzy snoozing a few feet away.

Christopher Trent came in the room and eyed them warily. "What's going on in here?"

Graham stood. "Mr. Trent, I hope you'll forgive me, but I've gotten a little ahead of myself. I asked Cassie to marry me before checking with you first..."

Cassie's dad looked surprised, but then he smiled. "What'd she say?"

Cassie jumped up and ran to him. "I said yes, Dad!"

"Well! Isn't that something!" Her dad hugged her close. "You be happy, honey."

"Oh, Dad. I *am* happy, I promise you."

"That's all that matters." Over her shoulder, her dad said to Graham, "You be good to her, you hear?" His voice was rough with emotion.

"I will, Mr. Trent. I swear it."

Cassie's dad joined them at the table. They talked for a few minutes, but it quickly became apparent that Graham and Cassie hadn't made plans beyond her acceptance of his proposal.

Olive said, "You two need a little time to yourselves." She turned to Cassie. "Go on to Graham's house. I'll milk the goats tonight and in the morning, too."

Cassie hesitated. "It's not right that you always end up taking care of the goats."

"Of course, it's right. I don't mind at all. Now, get a move on. You two have so much to talk about and for that, you need some time on your own."

"I love you, Mom. Thank you."

"Love you back. So much. You had me worried there for a little while." Olive's smile was wide and full of true satisfaction. "But just look at the two of you now."

Graham and Izzy waited downstairs as Cassie ran up to fill a backpack with what she'd need overnight.

A little later, at Graham's house, they ate leftover meat loaf for dinner. As soon as the meal was done, Graham scooped her high in his arms and carried her to his room.

They were awake late into the night. Not only did they desperately need to make love repeatedly, but as Olive had said, they had a whole lot to talk about, a lifetime together to plan.

Cassie explained that she'd never wanted to live anywhere but on Stargazer Ranch. He suggested that they could build themselves a house there.

She laughed. "I wasn't finished."

"Okay, then. Continue…"

"I never wanted to live anywhere but on Stargazer Ranch…until now. And now, Graham Callahan, I want to move in here, into this perfect log house on Callahan Canyon, with you."

That surprised him. "You sure?"

"Oh, yeah. I can still drive over to Stargazer to help out there four or five days a week. It's not that far away. But I do want to move the goats here, too. Is that too much?"

"'Course not. The goats need to be where you are. And I know just the place to put their new pen…"

She snuggled in closer and rested her head on his shoulder. "Let me guess. Out in back, across that meadow from the deck?"

"That's the spot."

"Perfect. There are a few shade trees and lots of brush back there. They'll be in goat heaven."

"All right, then," he said. "We'll make it happen."

"And you can help me build a better fence while we're at it—one that's Adelaide-proof, if you know what I mean."

"I do indeed."

"I love you," she whispered.

"And I love you," he replied as he tipped up her chin to claim a long, tender kiss.

* * * * *

Don't miss the next installment of the new continuity
Montana Mavericks: Behind Closed Doors

The Maverick's Forever Home

by USA TODAY *bestselling author Sasha Summers*
On sale August 2025, wherever Harlequin books and
ebooks are sold.